Ale

Paris Life

At Twenty

SALZWASSER
VERLAG

Alexandre Dumas

Paris Life

At Twenty

Reprint of the original, first published in 1863.

1st Edition 2022 | ISBN: 978-3-37500-478-1

Verlag (Publisher): Salzwasser Verlag GmbH, Zeilweg 44, 60439 Frankfurt, Deutschland
Vertretungsberechtigt (Authorized to represent): E. Roepke, Zeilweg 44, 60439 Frankfurt, Deutschland
Druck (Print): Books on Demand GmbH, In de Tarpen 42, 22848 Norderstedt, Deutschland

PARIS LIFE

At Twenty.

By ALEXANDRE DUMAS

LONDON

AMANDA.—THE CARNIVAL BALL.

AMANDA:

THE CARNIVAL BALL.

CHAPTER I.

A FIRST LOVE ADVENTURE.

ONE rainy evening in the month of February, 1846, I came to a grand determination—I decided that I would go to the Carnival Ball at the Opera House.

In consequence of this whimsical resolution, so suddenly made, I returned home at midnight and dressed myself. For this immolation I made myself smart, as Murat decked himself out for death.

Certainly, the opera-ball is a mournful affair enough; perhaps in no other saloon in the world does there assemble a like quantity of people for the purpose of wearying and saddening themselves; nevertheless, by an attraction that I have often yielded to without knowing wherefore, I went that evening, once more to tempt adventure—once more to mix in that assemblage of melancholy fools who, each week during the Carnival, keep a portion of the city awake through the whole night—that city which assumes to itself the title of the most intelligent of the civilised world.

I had made all these sage reflections whilst dressing myself; while, at the same time, I ventured to glance from the corner of my eye towards my bed, which seemed to smile at me with its turned down coverlet, as if to say to me, "Come; here is slumber and pleasant dreams;" and the book, just commenced, seemed to appeal to me from the bottom of its pages, "Stay; here is calmness and study."

I listened to the noisy rattling of the carriages, making the pavement ring joyously; I heard the merry shouting and the gay songs of those who, less palled than myself by the pleasures of the week, made a *fete* of this weekly pleasure; so I said to myself, in reply to the wily solicitations of my bed and my book, "Let us do as the others do; if we are with the sages, let us study their wisdom; and if we are among the fools, let us share in their folly."

And, after all, what is there to be done from Saturday evening to Sunday morning? If you chance not to go to the ball, you are sure the next day to wake up at an earlier hour than usual, and therefore leave home earlier than you generally do. Now, if the opera-ball is a wearisome affair, certainly the Sunday is a very insipid one. At the *cafe*, where you breakfast, instead of meeting the faces of friends of the night-revel, you are surrounded by people who on this day commit excesses beyond their daily habits of life, strolling about the streets like simpletons, or awkwardly sticking by the side of you from ten o'clock in the morning, with the same vacant staring face they have every day, and the coat of solemnity which they wear only on Sunday. These unknown gallants, for the most part, perhaps, excellent heads of families, have, with a full-blown visage, a tremendous laugh, which seems to ring from the coin in their pockets. It is very easy to see that, the week having been a good one with these tradesmen, the Sunday is, as a right, kept as a merry one.

Well, then, in passing your Saturday night at home, and in rising at ten o'clock on Sunday, you expose yourself to all these things, and join, without wishing to share or caring to understand it, in the laughter which is so utterly remote from your habit and your spirit that, instead of enlivening you, it only serves to make you sad.

Now, if there are two of you breakfasting together, you can remove to a distance from these unwelcome table-companions; you need not hear their talk; you can make, aside, remarks with all freedom, and less noise; but there are never two—you are always alone.

You leave home with the fixed intention of seeking one of your friends, and of breakfasting with him; but every door at which you rap remains closed, for all your friends, less virtuous than yourself, have kept the vigil of revels at the opera-ball, and they have not yet returned home; or, having returned late, they are yet asleep; and you have been too well brought up to disturb a man when he is eating, or to arouse a friend when he is asleep.

It only remains for you, then, poor abandoned soul, to

wander about alone, on the Boulevard, thus to await the hour for dinner—to meet with one of those thousand friends whose friendship constitutes in your estimation the beneficent air of the capital, and the eternal love of your mother-country.

When dinner-hour at length arrives, the first friend you light on comes towards you, yet rubbing his eyes, and appearing somewhat dissatisfied with having aroused himself so early on Sunday; you hasten to meet him; you fairly magnetize him, as the sparrow-hawk magnetizes the bird; then you fix on your prey, and no human force can make you abandon the arm that you have seized on.

Here is, word for word, the conversation that always takes place between you and your friend.

"Good morning, my dear fellow;" the other being fatigued, and consequently idle, replies to you only—

"Good morning."

"You are up?"

"Yes; at this moment."

"You have spent the night?"

"I've been to the opera; and you?"

"I?—no."

"That's true; I did not see you there."

"Were there many there?"

"It was full."

Your friend, who has now learned that you remained at home, and that naturally you did not see that he had been wearied out and disgusted with it, replies to you, partly from self-conceit, and to place himself in the exceptional position of a man who can be amused even at the opera—"Very much."

Then you feel furious with yourself for having given way to the temptations of your fire, of your chamber, and of your book; you even more than regret it; you are full of remorse at not having gone to this very ball, where, like your friend, you might have found amusement; and you promise yourself that henceforth you will not miss another.

The following Saturday you therefore once more return to the opera; but you leave it again as you have hitherto always left it, swearing that you will never return to it any more.

The result of all these many reflections is, that you decide that you must go to the ball, although it is true you are almost certain to be sick of it; but you have the consolation at least of being sick with some thousands of others, while, if you didn't go, you are quite certain, as shown by judicious reasons given, to be sick of yourself on the Sunday, and this, moreover, all to yourself.

Now, if there is a thing to avoid, it is that of being sick of yourself alone.

This truth is so incontestable, that Louis XIII. always gave himself up to *ennui* like a king who has a grand minister, and taking a gentleman of his court, would lead him into the recess of a window, saying to him, "Come and *ennui* yourself with me."

This evening, therefore, my resolution was decidedly fixed. I dressed; I went down stairs, to the envy of my porter, who looks upon the balls at the opera as the acme of terrestrial happiness; I got into a cab all of a quake. I arrived at the doors of the Opera in the Rue Lepelletier, and then, like Curtius, I precipitated myself into the gulf, which immediately closed around me.

I had been wandering about for perhaps an hour, sometimes in the *foyer*, sometimes in the lobbies, seeking amongst the visages surrounding me the face of some friend, when I perceived, leaning against the door of a box, a witty, intelligent fellow, whom I had not seen for six months past, at which time he was leaving for a tour in Italy.

The meeting was more than agreeable—it was unexpected. I placed myself exactly opposite to him, when I saw that he was chatting with a domino, who, on seeing me approach, was about to leave; using my discretion, I beat a retreat. My friend then saw me, and made a sign that he was coming to me, at the same time motioning me to wait.

I waited, proud and rejoiced at having found someone with whom to talk, and I looked with scorn upon the unfortunate ones who, solitary in that crowd, stared at all the dominoes, endeavouring to recognise or be recognised, and doing all in their power to create some intrigue.

Some moments after, the mysterious domino gave her

hand to Emmanuel (that is the name I will give my friend), then, bending forward, whispered a few words in his ear, and disappeared laughing.

Emmanuel followed her with his eyes, whilst, as approaching me, he murmured—

"What a problem a woman is!"

"Well," said I, on offering both hands, "where the devil do you come from?"

"From anywhere," replied he.

"You are returned to Paris, then?"

"These three months past."

"Then I will not ask you where you are coming from, but where you are going to."

"I am in love!"

"Then you are going to be mad."

"Oh, you know," added he, smiling, "in loving a woman, that woman becomes unto you the most distant of countries, inasmuch that she isolates you from all your friends, as from all your habits and customs."

"That which you tell me is full of truth; now, without being intrusive, may I know if that charming domino is the remote country which has and does separate us?"

"No."

"May I advance a supposition?"

"Do so."

"It seems to me, then, from the manner in which you chatted with her, that, if that is not a conquered country, it is a country you wish to conquer."

"It is a conquered country."

"Long since?"

"Since about two months."

"I am puzzled indeed."

"Why?"

"You have been in love three months past?"

"Yes."

"And during these three months, with the same woman?"

"Yes."

"And that woman is not the one with whom you were talking?"

"No."

"Then you are not so much in love as you said."

"Why not?"

"Because, if you were really so, you would not have quitted, were it even for a minute, the country to which you referred just now, to occupy another."

"It is not I who have been the seeker."

"Then I suppose you mean that an invasion has been made upon you?"

"Exactly so."

"Coxcomb!"

"I'll swear it is so."

"You are trying to draw me into an intrigue."

"Well, I came to the ball for that very purpose."

"Now, that's candid!"

"You have never been in an intrigue yourself, then?"

"Oh! yes, I have."

"Often?"

"Twice."

"And seriously so?"

"I believe you."

"For my part, at present I have only met at the opera-ball with women who took my arm, called me by my name, pretended they had met me on the Boulevard or at the theatre, and thus ended the interview and their story."

"Ah! with myself it has been quite another thing."

"Well, I'm listening."

"I think I must relate my adventures to you."

"Have you anything better to do?"

"No, nothing."

"Tell them to me, then; let's have them at once."

"You know as well as I do that the masked ball at the opera is the dream of college youths?"

"Ah, yes, indeed; how well I remember selling my dictionaries to come to the ball."

"And you amused yourself when you did come?"

"Go along with you! Every time that a woman came near to me I was all in a tremble lest she should speak to me."

"Then what did you come here to do?"

"Well, I really came only that I might be able to say the next day to my comrades that I had been to the ball, and thus assume to myself the air of a terrible reprobate."

"Well, then, my dear fellow, just have some admiration for me, for I really came here believing that I should find amusement."

"I admit yours was a much better object than mine."

"But, from what I shall relate to you, you will soon see that I was quickly filled with disgust. To my story: —One Saturday evening I succeeded in slipping away from home, and I hurried off to Babin's, and hired a costume."

"What was the costume?"

"A Turk's; oh! but, I assure you, it was that of a real Turk—a red turban, with a crescent on the top of it; a bright blue vest, made very short, and with a large yellow sun on the back; a loose pair of calico breeches; a waistcoat, just like the one worn by the actor Odry, in the *Saltimbanques*. I had thick double-soled boots; a false beard of horsehair, and a false nose of pasteboard; nothing, in fact, was wanting. I tied twenty francs in a knot of the corner of my pocket-handkerchief; and there was your friend complete!"

"You must have been all right, like that?"

"All right?—superb! I went to the ball; but, contrary to my expectations, I was not amused at all. I was alone, in the midst of a crowd where I did not know a single person. I was surrounded by women who called up my boyish blushes. Over and over again I thought to myself how this prank would have no other result for me save that of being punished by being kept in at college for three months. I was thus musing when a *debardeur*, with a soft, winning voice, half muffled by a fringed mask of black velvet, asked me why I seemed so melancholy in the midst of such general gaiety.

"I turned round, and examined my interrogator from head to foot. This woman had pretty little feet, nice, fine, delicate hands, and a profusion of dark black hair. I took the arm that she offered me, and at once I proposed to dance with her."

"Ah! you used to dance here?"

"No; but it was the only thing that occurred to me to say at the moment."

"Continue."

"She accepted my invitation, and we danced. My choregraphic education had been somewhat neglected; but I supplied all deficiencies by vigorous capers and grotesque contortions, which were to Terpsichore what Quasimodo is to Antinous. I had been told that the men who were held as the leaders of fashion did thus, and, therefore, unconsciously, I mistook all those tipsy gentlemen who flung their feet above their heads and cuffed everybody with their fists right and left as so many Montmorencys or Rohans, while at the same time they were so many 'barbers' clerks,' lovers for ten minutes of any girl. But, in reality, that which most flattered my vanity was that I had won a woman myself. This woman was at once to my imagination the most beautiful in the world; to me, that mask covered from my gaze a face before which that of the "Vierge a la Chaise" would pale, and that costume a form to make one forget the glory of the Venus de Milo. Well, I danced all night; but this was not enough; the point in question was to come to the definite and conclusive words of this stroke of good fortune. So I assumed to myself the subtleness of a Richelieu, and, with all the cunning I could summon, endeavoured to obtain the address of my fair unknown, and this with an unflagging perseverance, under which you would never have discovered a pupil of rhetoric. At length my importunity seemed to make way, and she spoke to me nearly in these words:

"'Sir, I really confess I have confidence in you.' An exclamation of joy escaped me as she spoke.

"'Tell me your name,' she continued.

"I told it to her at once.

"'Are you a relative of the deputy of that name?' she inquired.

"'Yes,' replied I, 'I am.'

"'Indeed?'

"'Yes.'

"'You'll give me your word of honour that that is the truth?'

"'It is, on my word of honour.'

"She appeared, so I thought, quite astonished and

delighted to have made the conquest of so distinguished a man. I leave you to think whether I didn't bridle up a little, and whether I didn't carry my head a little higher, when, all at once, she suddenly exclaimed, 'Now, I don't believe you.'

" 'I'll swear what I say is the truth,' I replied.

" 'Well,' she said, 'prove to me that you are really the person you say you are.'

" 'How can I do so?'

" 'Why, give me your card.'

" I haven't one,' said I. You can readily understand that at college we didn't have visiting cards.

" 'Well, then,' said she, tearing a leaf from a pocket-book, at the same time offering me a pencil—'well, then, write on that, that on your honour you engage yourself to do all that lies in your power to render me a service that I shall ask from you to-morrow.'

" This little incident seemed the more to add to the charms of the adventure, as blending with it the elements of the mysterious. I was young, you know, so I took the pencil and the paper, and I wrote unhesitatingly that which she dictated.

" 'And now tell me, where shall I see you to-morrow?' said I.

" 'In the opera passage,' she answered.

" 'But why not at your house?' I inquired, with the most insinuating tone I could find.

" 'Will you prove yourself worthy of that confidence?'

"'I give you my word of promise I will.'

"'Well, then,' said she, 'it is No. 32, Viellc Rue du Temple.'

"I confess that at the moment the address created in my mind an impression not altogether satisfactory; and the angel I had created to my imagination seemed to lose some portion of its divinity; but, after all, I was too far advanced to recede with any grace, so I reassured myself with the reflection that the house might be a beautiful one in spite of the street, or that the rooms of the interior might be agreeable in spite of the house, and, more, the lady might be charming in spite of the rooms. I took the address, therefore; and then, without having succeeded in persuading my fair incognito to disclose to me her features, I left the ball.

"I went to the costumier's; regained possession of my private clothes; and, not being able to go home, or to return at once to my college, I entered a restaurant, with all that swagger which comes to one with a first love-adventure."

CHAPTER II.

AMANDA RELATES HER MISFORTUNES.

"AT two o'clock I set out towards the Vielle Rue du Temple. To hasten the journey I got into a cab, which took nearly an hour to reach the place of appointment.

"At this distance of time I may have the candour to say that, in face of that house, so dark and disillusory in appearance, I was on the point of taking to flight, and thus losing all the adventure promised; just as a raw recruit who, on the battle-field, prefers the risk of being shot at once to the chance of coming to fighting. Still, as I had related the whole affair to the driver as we came along the route—for nothing induces openness like self-satisfied joy does, nor indiscretion like a cabman—a sense of shame mastered me, and I crossed the threshold of the house.

"If I had found the outside ugly, the inside was hideous; but I went on. Already at that epoch my character was resolute; this feature still remains to me my chief ornament. I looked about for the porter's room. I did not find it by sight; I discovered it by its savour. It was like the nest of an owl, perched in the angle of the most tortuous staircase you ever beheld.

"A head appeared at the window on the staircase, the

only head that could belong to such a box, so I leave you to fancy what it was like.

" 'Does Mademoiselle Amanda live here?" I asked.

" 'On the fifth floor," replied a sharp, sour voice, —'take the corridor to the right, turn to the left, and it's the fourth door after the second window.'

" At first thought it crossed my mind that I would conceal myself on the staircase a sufficient length of time to make my 'coachy' believe in the reality of my visit; but I soon found out that, if the sight, the touch, and the taste consented to this, the fifth sense, that of smell, obstinately refused. I chivalrously said to myself that, perhaps, after all, beauty might be found under the tiles, and love in the garret, so I went on. I reached the fourth floor. I began to fancy that the porter was making fun of me, for the stairs seemed to end there; but when, by degrees, my eyes became accustomed to the gloom, I discovered on one side an opening into darkness, as to a cavern.

" I entered, but only found my embarrassment increased. The door-keeper's directions became sadly jumbled together in my head, owing to the conflicting emotions that had accompanied my ascent. I found myself, not on a square, but on a cross-way, an alley or passage to the right, one to the left, one in front, another in the rear. After counting the windows and the corridors, I arrived, as I thought, at the door of my mysterious beloved one.

"With a beating heart I rapped at the door, saying to myself that if there was such a thing as justice in the world I was about to receive my portion, a portion to which such labour entitled me, half-way as I had already climbed to the sky; so I rapped at the door. It was opened by a little old woman, with light flaxen hair, and the absence of six front teeth unpleasantly perceptible.

"'Without doubt I have made a mistake, madame?'

"'Who are you inquiring for?' was her reply.

"A cold freezing shiver tingled through my veins. I seemed to recognise in the voice of that duenna the soft, sweet accents of my *debardeur*. I at once said—

"'Mademoiselle Amanda I am inquiring for.'

"'It is here,' she said, shutting the door as I entered. I breathed again; she had not said, 'That is my name.'

"My first thought on entering was to cast a glance round the chamber, with a discernment and penetration my peregrinations on the dim staircase had considerably augmented. I looked to see if there was not some second door that might open to a second chamber; but, keenly as I searched, I could discover nothing.

"The little old woman offered me a chair: I sat down, she did the same, and appeared to expect that I should commence the conversation.

"I didn't know what in the world to say. I would have sacrificed my uncle rather than have been where I was. I was about to open my mouth to say something, when, looking up, I saw on the bed the *debardeur* costume.

" 'Ah!' thought I to myself, 'she has gone out, and this old woman is charged to receive me;' as well as which, I urged to myself, in the face of ugly doubt, my unknown friend had brown hair, and this old woman's might once have been called blonde.

" Overjoyed by the mere supposition, I cried out, as if I considered that the old lady must be deaf—

" 'Mademoiselle Amanda!"

" 'It is I, sir,' she said, quickly.

" At college I had received plenty of hearty cuffs on my head, but never had I received one with the force of this reply. I was nearly fainting; I scarcely knew what I was doing; but was recalled from my confusion by hearing these words uttered in a tone of supplication;—

" 'Oh, sir, you are a man of honour?'

" 'Pray make yourself easy, madame!' I exclaimed

" 'And you would not deceive a helpless woman?'

" 'I'll take good care,' answered I, 'that I don't.'

" 'You are an honourable man, and Heaven will recompense you,' said she, looking at me with tenderness. I felt that my position was the most ridiculous that a man could be placed in.

" 'Pray pardon me, madame,' I at last said; 'but was it really you who were at the ball last night?'

" 'It was, sir.'

" 'In the costume of a *debardenr*?'

" 'Yes, sir.'

" 'And it was you who gave me your address?'

" 'Myself.'

" 'And you made me sign a paper?'

" 'Here it is.'

" 'Well, this is strange!' I exclaimed.

" 'What do you find strange in it?'

" 'That last night at the ball you had brown hair.'

" Amanda rose, and, taking up from the bed a black peruke that I had not noticed, she held it up before me. I was indeed confounded; my last hope had gone.

" 'I conceal my own hair,' said the old woman, 'so that I may not be recognised. Well, are all your doubts removed?' she asked.

" 'Yes, indeed, madame,' I mournfully replied.

" 'You appear dejected,' she said.

" 'I am on the contrary, as happy as it is possible to be,' I replied, with assumed carelessness.

" 'Oh! thank you for those words; they give me the fond hope that you will not abandon me.'

" 'What on earth can I do for you, madame?'

" 'It is in your power to give me happiness.'

" I began to believe she was going to ask me to marry her. I shuddered!

" 'Well, honestly, what do you think of me? how do you find me, sir?' she asked me.

" 'Why, madame, I find you a very agreeable person.'

" 'And do you think that a person might interest himself on my behalf without blushing?'

" 'Most certainly.'

" 'Then, sir, you must interest yourself on my behalf.'

" I told her I was ready to do so.

" 'Sir,' she resumed, 'I must beg you to understand that I am not a woman who attends masked balls. But I have suffered so much——'

" 'That you required a little diversion?'

" 'Oh! no, sir, you are mistaken; I was not at the opera-ball for pleasure, but for business.'

" 'Really, madame!' I exclaimed, taken aback.

" 'You shall soon understand me, sir. When you came to this house, you doubtless thought that my appointment was one of those rendezvous that are continually given at the opera-ball—a place for an amour?'

" I acknowledged that such was my impression.

" 'Sir,' she said seriously, 'you were mistaken.'

" I breathed more freely; but the mystery was not yet cleared up, and I said—

" 'Permit me to ask, madame, wherefore that *debardeur* costume?'

" 'Because that dress always appeared to facilitate the means of my obtaining that which I have never succeeded in gaining in any other attire. It is more than probable that, if you had not thought you should find a young and pretty girl disguised in that dress, you would not have come here, or have taken the arm that I offered you.'

" 'Oh! madame,' I cried, with mock gallantry.

" 'I must strive to interest you in what I have to tell

you; from having your written word that you would do all in your power to forward my interest, I should wish that you knew the history of my misfortunes.'

"'Pardon me, madame; though otherwise most anxious and willing to stay, I fear I have very little time to spare; if you will permit me, I will take leave of you now and return another day.'

"You can understand, my dear fellow, I was some way off becoming enthusiastic at the idea that I was about to listen to the narrative of the old lady's troubles. Unhappily for myself, I had fallen into sure hands; she wouldn't let me go. I was positively forced to give my attention, just as I might have had to have done in my uncle's chamber, had he been the one speaking to me.

"I resigned myself; if resolution and will can render one strong, certainly resignation renders one sublime! Of this I am sure, that, severe as was our head-master at college, had he known of that which I had thus to undergo and suffer, he would not have inflicted a further punishment.

"I am desirous that you should clearly understand the position of a rhetorician who, believing himself to be in good fortune, finishes, after eight hours of illusion, by finding that he has fallen into a trap.

"'Sir,' said Amanda, 'I was born in 1780.'

"It was now 1840, and I am sure that she concealed at least ten years; therefore I leave you to imagine how that avowal affected me.

"'Good heavens! madame,' said I, with so great an inclination to laugh, that it needed the recollection of my position to repress it, 'I have already had the honour to tell you that I am all attention; but it were needless to commence your story in that century, unless your misfortunes seized you in the cradle.'

"'Sir!' she replied, with an offended air, 'it is probable that if the woman was young and pretty you would not have made such an observation to her.'

"'I will only remark, madame, that, if the woman was young that relates her history to me, it is probable that that history would not have commenced in 1780, and would not promise to last so long as yours promises to do; and, therefore, there would be no need for the observation which I have taken the liberty to make.'

"I could see that the moment was approaching when she would create a perfect scene; this would have been more original than amusing, so I preferred to abstain.

"'Well, then, sir,' she rejoined, 'I will pass by my youth, although it would have been very sweet to communicate to you my dreams of girlhood; but I will relate to you the story of my sad existence, commencing only at the period of my marriage in '98.'

"'So young!' cried I; while at the same time I saw that I was only spared eighteen years of her history by her commencing from this per od.

"'Yes, sir; at the same time I was rather pretty,'

said she, gravely, 'to be married at that age. I pray that you will believe my word.'

"'I don't doubt a word, madame.'

"'I must make only one observation to you, sir,' she continued, 'which is, that since I have desired to make known the secrets of my life to you, you seem to use every endeavour to interrupt me; that is, doubtless, only to make me speak the longer.'

"'Oh! madame, can you entertain such an idea? It is easy to see that you do not understand my nature.'

"'Then will you listen to me?' As there appeared no means of doing otherwise, I consented.

"'Well,' she resumed, 'I was married, then, in '98, to a young man of nineteen; it was a marriage of love; we loved each other in spite of our parents. We loved one another to madness; we were so young, both of us! We had not a large fortune; myself, I had nothing; Anatole, the name of my husband, could obtain nothing from his parents; so that——"

"'So that, not only you had not a large fortune, but more, you were in the most profound misery?'

"'Yes, sir; you have guessed it exactly.'

"'Well, that wasn't very difficult to do; continue, madame, continue.' I was hoping by these interruptions to irritate Amanda, and thus to cause myself to be put out of doors; but I found this mode of operation failed utterly.

"'We loved one another so much,' she continued,

'that we forgot in one another's arms the stern realities and the material side of life. At that time there was a gentleman whom we knew who made pretty verses; he made four upon me that I still remember: shall I repeat them to you?'

"'Needless, madame;' and she continued—

"'It was for about a year that Anatole and myself enjoyed the sweets of Hymen; I cling to the expression of that poet; he became an academician. Well, one morning Anatole went out to buy some tobacco, and when he returned I was indeed changed.'

"'When he returned from buying the tobacco?'

"'Yes.'

"'How so—he returned then very late?'

"'Sixteen years after.'

"'Sixteen years after!' I exclaimed.

"'Yes, sir, sixteen years.'

"'What—are you the heroine, madame, of such an adventure as this?' I demanded, whilst unable to restrain myself from bursting into hearty laughter.

"'Yes, sir,' said she, with a deep sigh.

"'Really, it is very curious indeed.'

"'You clearly understand my story?'

"'Perfectly so.'

"'Well, then, sir, I repeat to you that I am the unfortunate person to whom befell that adventure.'

"'But that which I have heard does not,' said I, 'give me the completion of the strange adventure.' My curiosity had become excited; my attention was redoubled. 'What,' cried I, 'had your husband been doing all that time?'

" 'He had followed Bonaparte, in whose cause he was a fanatic; he had been at Austerlitz, where he had received the cross; in Russia, where he had had his feet frost-bitten; at Waterloo, where he had left an arm; it was in this state he returned to me.'

" 'He was yet more changed than yourself, then?'

" 'I did not recognise him. When he presented himself at our house I was with the poet of whom I spoke to you just now; I rose up, preparing myself to make a respectful salutation as to a stranger, when the supposed strange gentleman exclaimed to me—

" ' "He whom they call your spouse, my dearest Amanda!"

" 'He was unrecognisable, sir; instead of that pretty, beardless face, that made him resemble Phœbus, so the poet expressed it, I saw a kind of god Mars; that was also an expression of M. ——'

" She was about to tell me the name of her poet, when I interrupted her. I had a kinsman, an academician, from whom my family was alienated, and I trembled for fear she might name that relative.

" 'My husband,' continued she, 'was maimed; his face, reddened by fatigues and wine, was crossed with a sabre-cut; he wore great mustachios, like tusks, hanging down on either side of his mouth. He at once installed himself in my little room, with a volley of oaths enough to make the glasses rattle. I was utterly confounded; for, in the happiness his return gave me, I had thrown myself into his arms.'

"'Into his arm, was it not?'

"'Yes, sir,' replied Amanda, half-smiling at my malicious, cruel pleasantry; 'yes, sir, and he repulsed me —he cast me off. I called him my cherished Anatole —he did not respond to me; at length I flung reproaches at him; then he thrashed me, and from that day ever since he has not ceased——'

"'To thrash you?'

"'Just so, sir.'

"'He is yet alive?'

"'He is, sir.'

"'He is in Paris?'

"'Yes, sir.'

"'And he lives here?'

"'Yes, sir.'

"At this last 'Yes, sir,' I rose up and prepared to hasten from the room.

"'Where are you going?' cried Amanda, barring the door.

"'I must go,' said I, excitedly.

"'Why?'

"'Your Anatole frightens me.'

"'And you abandon me?'

"'Most decidedly so.'

" 'This is frightful!'

" 'Your husband will return?'

" 'Well, what then?'

" 'If he finds me here?'

" 'What then?'

" 'He will believe——'

" 'What will he believe?' exclaimed she, stretching out her hands like the Virgin on the little silver medals.

" 'That which is not the case.'

" 'But he knows that you are here.'

" 'He knows that I am here?' said I, with alarm.

" 'Yes.'

" 'Who has told him?'

" 'I have.'

" 'And why have you told him?'

" 'To pacify him, and to make him go out.'

" 'Well,' said I, 'I really don't understand you.'

" 'Sit down again, young man, and you shall understand all.'

" 'There was nothing else to be done; I sat down again; Amanda did the same."

CHAPTER III.

AMANDA IMPLORES TO BE SAVED FROM HER HUSBAND'S VIOLENCE.

" 'FROM the moment of his return,' resumed Amanda, 'our conjugal home became a hell. When he learnt that the Emperor had been sent to St. Helena, he became so furious that, not any longer content with thrashing me, he thrashed the poet, who consequently left off coming to see me; and with his withdrawal went our last resources, for he was as charitable as he was great. When at last the Emperor died in exile, Anatole created such an uproar and bedevilry in our quarter, that he was taken by the police and sent to prison for three months.

" 'I have sued in vain to get him an admission into the Hospital of the Invalides; the authorities were opposed to him, owing to his violence, and also on account of his too free and exaggerated opinions. To add to my misfortunes, he drinks all I can earn, and every day he returns home dead drunk; that is, when he does return; in short, sir,' concluded Amanda, throwing herself at my knees, in a flood of tears, 'Save me, pray save me!'

" I fancied that she would have risen up directly, so I did not speak.

" 'Then you have nothing to say to me?' she said, in a reproachful tone.

"'What, indeed, can I say to you, madame?' inquired I.

"'What can you say?—here you see a poor suffering woman, who casts herself at your feet, and you can find nothing to say to console and comfort her?'

"'You take me by surprise, madame, for I was ignorant that you were thus unhappy; and the costume in which I saw you that night——'

"'It was Anatole who made me wear that,' she interposed.

"'Anatole!' I exclaimed, with astonishment:

"'It was, sir.'

"'What interest or object had he in your doing so?'

"'He said to me, "Amanda, you must obtain some employment for yourself, by which we can live, since the means are denied to me. Dress yourself up in a *débardeur* costume—that's the taste of the day—and go to the masked ball; go to them every week until you meet with a deputy—the deputies can do anything;" so with our last resources I bought a costume, a wig, and a mask, and ever since the commencement of the winter season I have wandered through all the balls without being able to drop upon the deputy I seek. Yesterday fortune took a turn—I saw you; you had a distinguished air, the costume of a Turk that you wore excited my confidence; I said to myself—"Here now's an artless young man;" and I took your arm. You told me your name, and then I knew that your uncle was a deputy, and I came back from the ball to my little room, full of hope. I roused up Anatole from a fit of stupor; I gave him twenty francs to go and drink; I told him of the meeting I had had with you, and the visit that I expected, and I sent him away.

" 'He is about to return, sir,' she continued, after a pause, 'and if I have not a favourable reply to give him, he will kill me; save me, sir—oh! save me!'

" 'But what is it that I can do—what must I do?'

" 'You must get me,' she implored, 'you must get me a tobacco-license.'*

"Now, my friend," said Emmanuel, "can you understand such a conclusion? You go to the ball as a Turk; you fancy you have met with a piece of good luck; and the next day, when you hasten to the place of rendezvous, where you hope to find a grisette at the least, you encounter an old woman who implores you to procure for her a license to sell tobacco, and an old trooper, who throws himself at your knees, and completes this touching picture; for, by-the-bye, I am omitting to tell you that, at the moment the old woman was begging for her tobacco-license, her veteran husband,

* BUREAU DE TABAC of the original text, is, perhaps, more clearly conveyed by the phrase "Tobacco-license." The presentation to a Bureau de Tabac (a shop with permission or license to retail tobacco, of which the number is limited in Paris) is in the gift of Government, and is more usually accorded to the widows of soldiers, or the wives of disabled veterans.—TRANSLATOR.

Anatole, who, doubtless, for some minutes had been listening behind the door, dashed into the chamber, and flung himself at my feet, with a shower of those pitiful tears which inebriation so readily supplies, ceasing not all the time to repeat—

"Young man, young man, you who were dressed as a Turk, and who have an uncle a deputy, do not, do not abandon us.'

"I leave you to think where I wished myself. I raised up Anatole, who was indeed but badly supported on those feet frozen in Russia. I reseated Amanda; I affected to wipe away a tear with my handkerchief, and promised Anatole and his wife to use my best endeavours and interest on their behalf."

"'Did you remember to do so?" I asked Emmanuel.

"Not only did I remember, I did it. At the moment I was about to take leave of them, Anatole took me on one side and said to me—'Sir, I have not eaten anything to-day—lend me twenty francs.' I put a gold piece in his hand; he looked at it for a long time, turned it over with an inquiring look, and at length said to me, with a disdainful air, 'It's a Louis the Eighteenth!'

"'Well, won't you have it?' I said to him.

"'I should have liked a Napoleon better; but I'll go and change it, that I may not longer feel remorse.'

"The old soldier was turning to go out, when Amanda approached him, and said to him with a piteous tone—

" ' If you take away all that money, on what am I to dine?'

" ' On the remains of yesterday,' he replied.

" ' Yesterday !—yesterday we had no dinner at all.

" ' Silence ! hold your tongue, woman,' shouted Anatole, raising with a threatening air above Amanda the only arm he possessed. I sprung towards him, and arrested his uplifted arm half-way; he turned round and said to me—

" ' Mind you, young 'un, mind you see that she gets the tobacco-license; and take this word of advice from Anatole—don't you ever get married. The women, they are the ruin of us men.' He gave me an energetic shake of the hand, and with an unsteady step descended the five flights of stairs; but this he accomplished very easily, where I had had trouble enough in mounting.

" I remained alone with Amanda. The poor woman grieved me. I went up to her and gave her the last gold piece I had left, and said, ' I will not forget what you wish.' "

CHAPTER IV.

THE DEATH OF ANATOLE

"I RETURNED to college; my adventure, of course, became known to my comrades. Amongst them I was really run after. My father scolded me severely; but the paternal tempest, like all other tempests, subsided. I related my frolic to my uncle, who succeeded in obtaining an admission for Anatole into the Hotel of the Invalides, and procured a tobacco-license for his widow. I say his widow, for scarcely had Anatole become an inmate of the Invalides, from whence he was in the habit of coming to pillage his wife's till, than, one evening, returning drunk, as usual, he fell into a ditch, and with such violence that he never rose up again."

"Amen," said I.

"There's my history," said Emmanuel.

"And Amanda, where is she now?" I inquired.

"Amanda still lives on the bosom of pleasure and her tobacco-shop. You know me well enough to understand that after such a *debut* I swore to eternally abstain from coming to the ball at the opera."

"Bah!—abstain! And where do you fancy, then, you are to-night?"

"Oh! to-night, it's another thing; I am here by order."

"And the order is given by—— ?"

"By the domino that you saw."

"By the foreign country?" said I, laughing.

"Exactly so; and now adieu."

"What! you are going?"

"Yes."

"And my second history?"

"That one I will keep for another occasion."

"Why?"

"Because it is too long, and you have had enough of my talk to-night."

"Be assured I am now, as ever, ready to listen."

My friend Emmanuel led me from the *foyer*, saying—

"Let's go to supper; in that way you can take, at the same time, nourishment for body and mind."

"Your history is instructive, then?"

"Very instructive; it is a sketch from womankind. But you give me your word you will keep it secret?"

"I will."

Here is the story that he told it to me.

HENRIETTE, THE ARCHITECT'S WIFE.

HENRIETTE,

THE ARCHITECT'S WIFE.

CHAPTER I.

THE ARCHITECT'S WIFE.

"You know," said Emmanuel to me, when we were installed before the traditional partridge of the suppers of the Maison d'Or, (a celebrated restaurant and supper-house), "you know it is not my habit to tell false hoods?"

"That I know well."

"The history that you wish me to relate to you, then, is, I assure you, in all particulars a true one, although it may seem a very improbable one. However, as I have already told you, it is but a sketch, and not a finished picture; I shall give it you as a simple incident of my life without comment, and it will even be without an end."

"My dear fellow," I interrupted, "I had no wish to be at the ball to-night; I know not what prompted me to go—some good spirit, since it has led to my meeting with you. I expected to be wearied with *ennui*, as you know is our fate at these balls; and here not only do I meet with a friend whom I esteem, but a friend who positively has two unpublished histories; and you were wanting me to let that friend off before I had abstracted these two histories, from the first word to the last; that, however, couldn't be done, so resign yourself, and relate."

"Well, I'll commence;—

"One day I was searching for lodgings, and, strange to say, I met with the very rooms I desired in the Rue Neuve des Mathurins, on the fourth floor, with a view on one side over some pleasant gardens, the other side looking on the street.

"At this epoch my mind was full of sadness. I was quitting a house where I had been very happy indeed, and where daily I recalled in my musings the trace of events that had passed, and that would never more return. This it was that made me sad—as the sight of a casket bereft of its jewels.

"I was in love; and in love, as we always are, too late or too soon. You know well enough how our college-life warps the best feelings of the heart; you know what impure theories are there promulgated. Every youth who leaves our college is a sceptic by fashion; and at that age we think there is nothing of intelligence or of wit in the world, save with those who neither believe in God nor in woman. I was among these, or I schooled myself to believe that I was. My boyish view saw the world through the gratings of the college, and I believed it to be a world of beauty; but I lent myself to see it through the stories of my comrades, and then I despised it. You know what these comrades are; you know the society they frequent on the Sunday instead of being with their families, or going away into the country, to be amongst the trees and the flowers—that eternal family of the heart and soul. Constituting themselves the apostles of vice and corruption, they bring back for the Monday's recital some story of dissipation, wasting the heart and enervating the sense. I followed the common law; I mixed with the group of the faithful who listened to their oracles; and I carried away with me my large share of scepticism and disgust.

"I fancied that these principles contributed to make me some Bassompierre, some Lauzun, some Richelieu of the nineteenth century. I even mourned for that epoch wherein Marie de Medicis was the mistress of the Premier, Madame de Montespan of the Second, and Madame de Valois of the Third; until, at length, I was quite astonished that even virtue of the slightest shyness or modesty repulsed me rudely when I made advances with my barrack deportment.

"Meanwhile, I gave myself up to the vulgar pleasures of my companions; pleasures that cannot even be called love-affairs, and which pass away even from recollection, leaving no more traces on our heart than the wing of the bird leaves upon the air. These *liaisons* completed my education, and confirmed my theories. I must, however, avow that I have sometimes remarked on the faces of those young girls who pass for indifferent, a certain melancholy amid their gaiety, which seemed the last reflection of their past, the last regret of a happiness that had flown.

Observe, I do not make myself the apologist of vice or debauchery: yet, while granting there is among these abandoned ones degraded hearts on which the ray of hope and love has never fallen, and on which it can never descend, still there are many among them whose gaiety s but a fiction, whose indifference is but falsehood—in whose eyes I have beheld tears, when inadvertently in talk I have chanced to raise a corner of the veil which revealed to them a glimpse of the sacred happiness of the family hearth; and, believe me, so long as you see a woman weep, do not despise her, do not wholly cast her off, for she yet holds to Heaven by something; and if she has not the soul of the Virgin who prays, she has, perhaps, the repentance of the Magdalene who suffers.

"I was at this time, then, what grand-parents call a 'bad character.'

"In the midst of my orgies—which consisted of a supper, and hiding myself at the back of a stage-box, behind some pretty faces, a practice which constitutes the refinement of corruption—in the midst of my orgies a woman became passionately fond of me. This time it was a real piece of good fortune.

"You must know that my uncle, the one who obtained

the tobacco-licence for Madame Anatole, was an old libertine, who had retired from gaiety on account of his lease having expired. He had wished to renew it, but his doctor had warned him that in such case a general break up would ensue. He loved me very much, and wished to snatch me from the bad habits in which he had left the two-thirds of his fortune and the three-fourths of his health. With this object before him, he resolved to present me in that which he called the real world. He had for a friend Leopold C——, the great pianist, whose house was one of the most amusing in Paris, and whose wife one of the most distinguished in the capital—that there is, indeed, since she is yet living. M. C—— received at his house that intelligent artist society which is the moving *controle* of all Parisian reputations. It has a horror of the middle class citizen ; is pitiless to all things commonplace ; talent enters into it without announcing itself, whilst cyphers dance attendance in vain. All the familiars of that house stood for something by themselves individually ; not one but had produced his book, his opera, his picture, his statue, his engraving, his saying, his sensation.

"Every Tuesday the saloon of that house buzzed like a hive ; and what honey they made there ! A swarm of young and lovely women assembled at that house ; and the epigrams, the coquetries, the pearled laughter, the wit, under every form, which bounded from one end of the saloon to the other, as a shuttlecock from the battledores of children! Each one that came was expected to contribute his share; and it flashed upon me, in setting my foot in that *reunion*, that I had but just the time to cast away and leave behind me at the door my false theories of immorality. I could not, however, strip them off quick enough, and I retained a certain feeling of defiance, not of the wit of these ladies, but of their virtues.

"My uncle was adored by all the friends of M. C——. I was myself received, I might almost say, with injustice, for I was not made to pass the ordinary tests. The facility thus accorded somewhat humiliated me; I felt that it was considered that I was not very brilliant, and, therefore, must not have obstacles placed in my way, from respect for my uncle. I was mistaken, however; they paid no attention to me, for the simple reason that everybody who gained admittance there was considered at home.

"At that time I had plenty of spirit, so I at once wished to test my strength as soon as possible. After the partial presentations, instead of remaining fastened to the side of my uncle, I first skirmished about the saloon with some of the groups; then, growing bolder, I threw myself bravely into the general *melee*. There was a discussion going on; at this moment I no longer know what it was about; all that I remember is, that my opinion was asked for, and that I coolly developed it in the centre of a silent circle not wanting in due solemnity. I carried my head up I assure you. It was victory or death. I found, as I then thought, some happy words, some adroit paradoxes. From time to time I could hear the master of the house saying to my uncle, 'He is charming—charming, indeed!' To be brief, at the end of my peroration I landed amidst approbation almost unanimous. From that moment I was classed among the amusing."

Emmanuel, at this point of his story, paused with a deep sigh.

"What ails you now?" I said to him.

"Nothing. I regret that house."

"It no longer exists, then?"

"Yes, it exists; but I no longer go there."

"And why?"

"Because I have become an imbecile."

"And why have you become an imbecile?"

"Ah! there it is! You will know this soon enough. Let us return to my history.

"My heart was yet fluttering with my little success, for I felt that I was playing a large part there for a juvenile like myself, when the door of the saloon opened, and the domestic announced—Madame d'Harnebey."

"The architect's wife?"

"Yes—you know her?"

"Only from reputation; I have never seen her. Some say that she is very pretty; others that she is very ugly; but all agree in saying that she is, or rather that she was, a little light, for I have not heard her spoken of for some time past."

"You will see. First let me tell you she is the most beautiful creature I have ever met. Nothing in the world can convey to you an idea of the pride of her step, of the distinction of her outlines, of the happiness of her postures. The reason that her beauty has been often questioned—nay, more, denied—is that she had hair of the colour which both the browns and the blondes can speak against—hers was auburn; if you do not like auburn, tell me, and I will not continue the portrait."

"I adore it—that is, auburn; but let us clearly understand one another—"

"I know what you are about to say to me—'There is auburn, and there is red;' Madame d'Harnebey's hair, a yard and a half in length, was of the tone of English gold, and undulating naturally; the eyebrows and the eyelashes almost black, the eyes of Sevres blue; the profile one to be struck in a medal; the lips ardent; and the teeth, white as pearls; the comparison is old, but it is still the best. Imagine to yourself, then, how, when this woman entered, it seemed to me that all the others quivered like phantoms, and receded to the walls like the figures on tapestry. That woman overwhelmed all with her appearance; her costume had the audacity of an incontestable superiority, to which everything is permitted. She wore the veritable head-dress of a *bacchante*, made with acanthus and vine-leaves, with berries of the grape mixed with the silken undulations of her hair, which fell behind half-way down her neck in a voluptuous fold, from which escaped some provoking ringlets. She entered without removing the mantle which covered her ball-dress. This mantle was a *bournous* of red cashmere, with a simple border of gold. She walked straight to the mistress of the house, as if there had been but her alone in the saloon, and offered a hand, gloveless, without rings, white, supple, and which, with its rosy fingers, lightly bending at the tips, seemed formed expressly for the caresses of love. In this movement she discovered a beautiful bare arm, without other ornament than a large gold circlet. Powerful magic of beauty! From the entrance of that woman there, all the assemblage lapsed into silence. It remained for them to look and to admire; and, in looking and admiring, I began to understand the Pagan of antiquity, unto whom form was a kind of religion.

"All the men drew close about the new arrival with a murmur of admiration; whilst the object of it deigned to remember that there were other women present, and smiled and offered them her hand.

"'How beautiful you are, my dear madame; and this is for us?' inquired Madame C——.

"'No; it is for the Ottoman ambassador.'

"'Ah! that is true; I remember there is a ball this evening at the Embassy.'

"'And I am come to show myself before going there.'

"'Take off that *bournous*, then, that the beautiful robe may be seen.'

"Madame d'Harnebey undrew one of the golden tassels, and the mantle, gliding over her round shoulders, fell with its weight, she not making an effort to retain it. I was near to her; by a mechanical movement I stretched forth my hands and received the mantle in my arms. She thanked me with a slight movement of the head, fixing her eyes for an instant upon my face, which was unknown to her. I felt myself blush. She smiled. That blush of a boy of eighteen years, who has not too simple an air, said more to her, and pleased her more, than all the compliments from people who knew her. That which most charms women habituated to praise is the artless expression of admiration that their beauty evokes, even where it is coarsely spoken. I have heard women of the world say that the compliments which have the most genuinely flattered them were those spoken by men of the people whom they have passed in the streets, and who praised them in vigorous language.

"Now, the woman I had under my eye was a real woman. Her *bournous* fallen, she appeared to us under another aspect. Lace, silks, ribbons, gold, pearls; and, under all that, thanks to the sobriety of the lines, thanks to the harmony of the folds, a beautiful figure could be divined, supple and firm.

"The murmur of admiration beeame a concert. The reputation of the beauty of Madame d'Harnebey was so well established in this house that the women themselves no longer dreamed of contesting with her, even when her eccentricity presented itself, as on that day, under a costume more or less open to criticism.

"During this time her husband looked at her with the others, but without the least pride, or more as a man who, having his personal value, does not need the beauty of his wife to make himself remarkable. M. d'Harnebey was forty-five years of age. He passed for a married philosopher; occupied with immense public works, it was said that he left all liberty to his wife to do just as she liked; and it was reported that she abused it. A circumstance that I had quite forgotten all at once crossed my mind when I had looked at Madame d'Harnebey. Two years previous I had been to Marseilles, with my uncle, who was leaving for Italy; I accompanied him as far as on board the steamer, and I returned to the shore with some of our friends.

"'Your uncle is lucky indeed,' said one of them.

"'How so?' I inquired.

"'He will make the passage with Madame d'Harnebey, who is going to join her husband at Rome.'

"'Who is that Madame d'Harnebey?' I asked. They explained this to me in adding—

"'In twenty-four hours you will have one aunt more.'

"I did not then know Madame d'Harnebey; I had never seen her. I did not attach any great importance to this circumstance. My uncle returned from Genoa; but the incident had quite left my memory. I never even thought to speak to him about it; until thus meeting with the heroine it all recurred to my mind, and I said to myself how lucky my uncle must be; for I no longer doubted that the insinuations of our friends might have been realized; and I was confirmed in my convictions when I saw my uncle approach Madame d'Harnebey, and take her hand with an air of familiarity. I seemed to see the same recognition in the pressure of the hand as in the expression of the eyes. For a moment they chatted together.

"'And you are going to dance with that robe?' said my uncle.

"'Yes.'

"'Mark my words—after the first waltz it will be in pieces.'

"Madame d'Harnebey did not directly reply, but she inquired—

"'Do you still waltz?'

"'Sometimes,' said my uncle.

"'Well, then, my dear C——,' she said to the master of the house, 'put yourself to the piano, play a waltz for us of ten minutes, and I'll wager to dance to the end without disarranging one fold of my dress.'

"Thus speaking, she held out her arms, and placed herself by the side of my uncle. C—— sat down to the piano; every one looked. It was reputed that all this woman did was accepted as perfect.

"'Oh! I no longer waltz well enough for you,' said my uncle, gaily; 'but, stay, here is my nephew, who is an excellent waltzer, and who I now present to you; I defy you to fatigue him.'

"'We shall see,' she said, smiling. We commenced; at first we made the tour of the saloon two or three times alone; then some others, allured by the music, followed us; and soon there was not one woman left sitting—all that were young revolved. The waltz lasted ten minutes.

"'You see?' said Madame d'Harnebey to my uncle, as we stopped; 'intact!'

"In reality, any one would have thought she had just arrived. Her robe was as fresh, her tint as rose, her respiration as calm as when she entered—only—ah! only—the movement of the dance imparted an indescribable charm—a charm that I had never beheld before. I was dazzled, intoxicated; I could but follow and gaze on, led as by enchantment. I went to my uncle, and partly disclosed to him what I felt; and I could not refrain from saying to him—

"'You must, indeed, be happy.'

"'Why so?' said he.

"'To have been the lover of that woman.'

"'I?—never!'

"'And—do you remember—the passage from Marseilles to Genoa?' I stammered out.

"'Oh!' said he, 'I was unwell all that voyage; indeed, she made great fun of me.'

"'Indeed?'

"'Yes.'

" 'Then there is nothing in the story?'

" 'Nothing.'

" I was ready to dance with joy. Madame d'Harnbey passed near when we were talking.

" 'Do you know what my nephew confesses to me?' said my uncle to her.

" 'Tell me.'

" 'He says that he is mad after you.'

" She turned away laughing, but without reply For myself, I blushed all over; it was the second time I had blushed. Ten minutes after she was gone. She had left for the ball at the Embassy; she was no longer there; but her presence remained before my eyes always: it moved with me everywhere; I thought only of her all the evening, and I dreamt but of her all the night.

" Was I in love? No. It was only that that woman had deeply influenced my imagination. A strange mixture of feelings by turns took possession of my mind; for some moments I seemed positively to detest her; I really should have wished to do her an injury. She occupied my thoughts too much and too little. The question was to see her again, but how? and then, what to say to her? I could never have the courage to make love to her—I dare not. Well, then, where were all my infallible theories? I saw that after all my pretensions I was yet but a scholar, and it was from her that I must learn.

" Meanwhile, I did not see her again. The springtime was come, and the reunions of Leopold C—— were banished to the winter following. For these, therefore, must I wait, or it were needless for me to entertain dreams of her. But my uncle was an arch fellow; he had seen through all, and planned matters without my suspecting him in the least, and, indeed, without appearing to be in the least mixed up with them. One morning, breakfasting with me, he said—

" 'I met Madame d'Harnebey yesterday.'

" 'Ah!'

" 'Yes; and we are to dine with her to-morrow.'

" At this dinner there were only M. d'Harnebey, his wife, their two children, my uncle, and myself. She studied me all the time, without appearing to do so. On leaving the table she spoke in an undertone with my uncle, but I felt quite certain that I was the subject of her conversation.

" Later in the evening some people came. Madame d'Harnebey's manner was abstracted and absent, and at times full of sadness. I certainly held no part in that abstraction, for nothing of that sadness remained in the stolen glances with which I saw she looked at me from time to time. Some heart-melancholy had, doubtless, with sure blow, but recently crossed the apparent lightness of this woman. She perhaps sought in me the possibility of a consolation. Such was the impression I carried away from that evening. Three days after I was about to pay my visit.

" 'You will say to Madame d'Harnebey,' said my uncle, " that I should have accompanied you, but that it is impossible to-day.'

" It was evident, in reality, that he intended that I should visit her alone. I went; she had gone out, M. d'Harnebey also. I left my card. The day following I received a letter, in which she expressed her regrets at not having been at home when I called, and she also mentioned the hour at which she was sure to be found. I went at the hour named. She was alone; she received me, as I thought, somewhat with indifference; our conversation flagged. I said nothing that was good. It was the interview of a woman *blase* and a clumsy juvenile wooer. In the salutation of the hand which she gave me when I took leave of her, it seemed to me this phrase was conveyed—' Well, decidedly, this will never do.'

" I confess I left humiliated. Some days after, my uncle said to me—

" ' Emmanuel, you are indeed a boasting simpleton.'

" ' How so?' said I, not a little displeased.

" ' You wish to be the lover of the most beautiful woman in Paris, and you do not know how to win her.'

" ' Who is that, then?'

" ' Madame d'Harnebey.

" ' Who has said that to you?'

" ' Herself.'

" ' Herself?'

" ' Yes; I had said every imaginable fine thing of you;

it was a good moment—a most auspicious moment. She had just broken off with Jules de Vercy——'

"'The painter?'

"'Yes.'

"'And now?'

"'Now it is too late—they are reconciled again.'

"I was furious; but with assumed indifference I said to my uncle, 'Well, what is that to me? she doesn't please me.'

"'Well, all I can say is, you please her, and I am sure that she has only been reconciled with Jules because you have not known how to take his place.'

"'She must always have a lover, then?'

"'It appears so.'

"What was to be done? To return to Madame d'Harnebey was to run the chance of being laughed at; on the other hand, not to go there was voluntarily to make myself forgotten. This superb coquette must have found me supremely simple. I was keenly stung; I had, therefore, a revenge to take. I must gain that woman, less to *have* won her than to be able to say I *had* won her.

"It was quite evident that, when I had visited Madame d'Harnebey, she had thought no more about me since the evening of the soiree. She had met me just at the termination of one of those *liaisons* which arise from the relations of the world in which she lived; a position without novelty, and which makes the lover a second husband, who in Paris society is attached to marriage as the shadow is to the body. I had betrayed by my looks, and afterwards by that speech which my uncle had repeated to her, the impression she had produced upon me; something of youth had arisen within her. A light play of illusions had breathed over her heart, and she had said to herself, 'Here is a soul all new and full of freshness, in whose glow it will be a delight to revive.' But the feeling that awoke in her for me fell to slumber aga n, as she turned to the influence of another love. The half-opened door of her heart, by which I could have entered, was again closed, and there was an end of it with me.

"There had been, however, a moment in her mind when I had ceased to be a stranger to her. I had played a part, though but for a minute, in her life; I had been a possibility in the eventualities of her future. To myself, therefore, it was more than necessary to recover a footing upon the ground where I had slipped on first trial.

"I came to the decision that I would write to her. I wrote to her; it was stupid to do so, but I believe that in love the stupid means are the best. She repeatedly replied to me that she did not understand my letters; but she said she would not ask me for anything better than that I would come to explain them to her.

"From the moment that she thus accepted the com bat, I knew that she was certain to be vanquished. I hastened to her. She asked me why she had not seen me for so long a time. I made the most of the situation; it was a justice to be rendered to myself. I replied to her, apologising for my frankness, that I had had the hardiness to love her, but that, on hearing the return to her house of one whom I had believed banished, I had abandoned myself to despair.

"'Why have I written to you?' I resumed, at the end of this discourse to her; 'I should not know how to explain it; it was an act above the control of my will. Do not pardon me, madame,' continued I; 'say what you will of my audacity; perhaps your censure will restore me to reason,' etc., etc. You can easily guess all that I could say on that text; a veritable cherub could not, I assure you, have discoursed better.

"She listened to me, smiling. We made love to the full, with the traditional mannerism which is ever the prelude to this kind of love-affairs. She gave me permission to write to her, under the pretext that she was dull, and that it would amuse her; and she promised to reply to my letters. I wrote at once, as soon as I returned home. My letter was that of a country coxcomb. The next day I received this reply:—

"'You are a clumsy one. The first attempt goes for nothing; begin again.' It was impossible for me to put more grace into them. I tore up my letter that she had sent back to me, and I wrote her another. This time her reply was—

"'That is better—continue.'

"From this moment I had nothing more to do than go straight on; the way was revealed to me.

"Have you a good memory for dates?" said Emmanuel to me, diverging from his story. "I have a good one myself, and shall ever remember the 11th of April, 18—. The season of the year was advanced; the lilacs were in flower. She came to me dressed as for a *fete*. I had waited for her for an hour, and my heart had been beating as though it had wagered to beat in one hour the pulsations of a day.

"'I thought I should not have been able to come,' said she, raising her veil, as she entered my room.

CHAPTER II.

ON WOMAN AND FRIENDS.

"OH! friends! friends!" cried Emmanuel, again interrupting the thread of his story; "if, however, that name can be given to those parasites of sentiment with which a young man of twenty is surrounded—friends! those enviers of your glory, of your fortune, or of your wife, who, in associating their name with yours, have ever the second thought that some benefit will return from so doing, and that the world will suppose them to hold in your house the position which theya spire to, and which, indeed, like Tartufe, they will sometimes take; friends! those idlers who constitute themselves the guardians of your honour, the judges of your conscience, who marry you, who ruin you, who make war upon you, without your consent, and who cover themselves at once with that phrase, 'I have done that which I consider to be right.'

"Therefore, Orestes and Pylades excepted—they must be kept for comparison—one ought never to speak of friends, and the word should be erased from the language; above all, in the vulgar sense in which it is now received. The reason that will make friendship exist till the end of time, in name, at least, and by custom, is, that it has on the one side the air of protection, and that with this protection it dominates. Now, the greatest vanity in man is domination.

"I abuse by digression, but what would you have? I cannot, when I fall upon a paradox so foolishly accepted by men, resist the impulse to cry out against it.

"I had 'friends,' then, at the time I speak of. Now, these friends, to whom formerly I had been in the habit of giving all my time, and to whom I recounted all my actions, no longer found me at home when they came, for my days were nearly always passed in visiting the country with Madame d'Harnebey.

"By the way, it really must be acknowledged that there is in woman, whatever be the class, an eternal thirst after the magnificent works of creation. There are very few women, however lost they may be, who are not influenced and moved by the beauty of sunlight, of the flowers, and of the fields. The immensity of plain, the mystery of woods, isolate them from their present, and awaken their better natures; when in the midst of the peaceful country, steeped in its silence and tranquillitv, the shadows of their past recede to a horizon so distant, so remote, that they become difficult to distinguish, and oftentimes are forgotten wholly. It is very rare at such a time that they do not belong, life and soul, to the one who shares with them this presence of happiness, and that the man on whose arm they lean be not the chosen of their hearts. It is then that the heart of the woman realizes that fantastic dream of which her nature has such incessant need; the withdrawal with him whom she loves to the bosom of that mother nature, at once clear, shining, and mysterious, whose beneficent serenity breathes of pardon, and in the midst of which she would die at the end of fifteen days' solitude were the man weak enough to accept such sacrifice.

CHAPTER III.

A CONFESSION.

"In the end, my friends—since I must call them by this false name—my friends rendered me very unhappy. They were unceasingly questioning me:—

"'What is become of you? One never finds you at home now. Where do you spend all your days? They say this; they say that. You have a new mistress, then? They will have it that it is Madame d'Harnebey. Is it true?'

"I only replied to them—No. She is no longer young. She has red hair. She is ugly. She has no heart. She is the acquaintance of such a one. She herself has related to me such and such things about him.

"You see, I had not a heart sufficiently courageous to place myself above all their attacks. It seemed to me that I should appear ridiculous did I acknowledge myself to be in love, and also if I should take the part of this woman. On the other hand I was not displeased that they should know that I was her lover; so, to conciliate all these little wretched vanities which tortured me, I found, in my weakness, nothing better than to compromise Madame d'Harnebey. I fancied myself thus to have the air of a great rake, but it was, indeed, an assumption.

" 'Yes, she is my mistress,' said I; 'but she has run after me, not I after her. I could not play the Joseph. I do not love her; but as well her as any other.' And I had the villany to show her letters; and at our suppers I toyed and played with her name. I went so far, when my friends assembled at my rooms, when at the same time this poor lady was there, as to open the curtains of the apartment in which she was awaiting me. I felt and knew that this was cowardly conduct, for I had nothing to reproach her with, and yet I dared not to love her frankly and openly. I even went so far as to stigmatize as a crime her having listened to me so quickly. I presumed to see in this one of a series of habits. Two or three times I was cruel enough to speak of this to her.

" 'You are right,' she would say to me; 'but it is not for you to cast reproaches.'

" I spoke to her of her former love engagements. I repeated to her the names which idle rumour coupled with her own.

" 'For what good object do you talk to me of the past?' said she. 'It is not generous, and, moreover, it does not concern you; you are too young to understand all the reasons that make the heart of a woman vacillate until it has found its true place. I ask you, since you have known me, have I had the air of a coquette? Am I not wholly yours? But, remember, I am your mistress, I am not your wife. Yours is not the right to demand account from me, save of the present; the rest belongs to my husband.'

"There was no reply to make to this; I only knew that in the depth of my heart I was in love with her, and yet without wishing to avow it; and so by consequence I was positively becoming jealous.

"It is a strange mania, that retrospective jealousy. No sooner is the heart of a woman won, but from that moment we make a descent upon that portion of her life in which we have not the least right—her past. We rake it up, we comment upon it, we sift it, we calumniate it. It needs must that she should never have loved before, that she should have divined that one day she would meet with one's self, we who are not worth more, whoever we may be, than those she has listened to before; if she were that which one desired her to be, she would not have listened to one, she would be virtuous, and we should have despaired before her indifference instead of being tormented in our success. But we learn the truth of this but too late. I am paid to day in my repentance, in having overlooked this. I could have been so happy, and I should be yet; whereas——"

Emmanuel lapsed into a moment's silence, then continued—

"All things conjoined to make my existence delightful. I was young. I had my liberty, and as much money as I desired.

"At the time I am speaking of, my lodgings were in

one of the only quarters in Paris where there are still gardens. They were rooms that my mother had chosen for me, that her love had adorned and screened as a cradle, and had sanctified and perfumed as a chapel. Here, at noon, it was my custom to place myself at my window, and then some instants after I could see in the street the flutter of the robe that I was expecting. Scarcely had the approaching visitor caught sight of me than her step was hastened, and then, as though fearing by the direction of her look some one might guess of whom she was thinking, and to whom that look was directed, she would turn away her head, as with an air of indifference, but from which, nevertheless, escaped some confidential glances.

"Then I listened as I heard her ascend the three flights of stairs. I went to meet her, and then we remained thus two or three hours together; or we slipped away like two schoolfellows, and, as. I said before, hastened away into the green sunny country.

"The days that she could not come and see me she always wrote to me. Thus, you see that I ought to have been happy; but our poor human nature is at once so base, so ambitious, so wanting in faith, that it doubts all, and is contented with nothing.

"When this woman proffered me her hand, and seated herself by my side, instead of loving her in return for the love she showered upon me; instead of kissing her little feet, which for me quitted their velvet slippers and their silken cushions ; instead of thanking that heart beating with emotion ; instead, in short, of prostrating myself before this being who, whilst seeing me ncither as a cipher nor wicked, consented to make known to me the treasures of her soul and the revelations of her love —do you know what I did? Well, then, like the cruel, heartless children who catch the summer birds but to tear out their feathers, and not that they might listen to their songs, so did I torture that woman. I tore from her one by one the bright illusions she had created to herself of me ; and the smile that rose to her lip turned back again to tears in her eyes and blushes on her brow.

CHAPTER IV.

A LOVERS' QUARREL.

"For nearly three months did life pass in this way. Each morning she sent to me flowers, or a letter, and during the day she came to talk or work near to me; when, one Sunday—I shall ever remember it—I went to dine in the country with a 'friend,' and, at the dessert, the conversation fell, were it by chance, or intentionally, on Madame d'Harnebey.

"The young fellows dining there may or may not have known of my position with her; of this I am ignorant. All I can tell you is, that, doubtless at a moment when she was thinking only of me, and awaiting the morrow, these fellows were busying themselves a great deal about her at the dinner table, at St. Mande; this time it was not only of the past that they spoke in reference to her life, but of the present.

"At length one of these men actually affirmed, on his word of honour, that within eight days past that woman had been the mistress of one of his friends. I turned pale as death. One instant, rapid as a thought, flashed over me the longing to throw the lie back in the face of the man who made the assertion. Then that pride which drove Lucifer from Paradise took possession of my soul, and the fear of ridicule, so ridiculous in itself, smote me back into silence.

"I listened with suppressed anguish and anger to the details of the story. Nothing, it seemed to my excited spirit, was wanting; I had been deceived. Blinded by anger against all reason, I did not reflect. I never even thought how impossible was the story that I heard narrated; and that during the hours that it was asserted that my mistress held rendezvous with another she had always been with me.

"I returned home. I sat down at once and wrote a shameful letter to that woman—I discarded her as false. I slept but little that night. The next day, however, were it by custom, were it from presentiment, I awaited noon with impatience. I did not place myself, as usual, at the window, or rather, I did not place myself so that I could be seen. I closed the Venetian blind, through the bars of which I looked down into the street.

"I saw her come; she was not dressed in white nor in rose colour, but was dressed in black. She looked up at my window, and this time, so different to her wont, w thout in the least disguising the action; then she entered the house. With ear close to the door, I listened breathlessly, as she mounted the stairs. I was even half longing to add to her sufferings by not opening the door to her. My thoughts struggled violently with one another, without the least order in the chaos of my mind. But,' urged I to myself, 'if a woman that you do not love has influence thus to overthrow you, in what state would you be cast, then, by a woman that you really love?'

"She rapped at the door; I opened it. She was pale as the dead; she passed in; she swept before me without uttering a word, with a sad, yet, at the same time, a proud look. I went up to her. She was evidently a prey to violent inward agitation. She sank rather than sat upon a chair. She tore asunder the strings of her bonnet, and, bursting into tears, she covered her face with her hands.

"'May I know, madame, to what I owe the honour of your visit?'

"'To what?—to the infamous letter that you wrote to me yesterday,' she replied; 'I now return it to you; for you ought to repent of it as for a base and cowardly action.'

"'I never repent of that which I do,' I said, in my vanity, 'for I do nothing without reflection.'

"'Then you really believe,' she said, all at once hurriedly drying her tears, 'you believe that which you have written to me in that letter?'

"'I do, madame.'

"'And if I swear to you that it is false?'

"'I shall believe it still.'

"'And if, also, I prove to you that that man whom you name in your accusation does not know me?'

"'I shall believe it still.'

"'And if, also, I prove to you that that man whom you name in your accusation does not know me?'

"'I shall believe it the same as ever.'

"'Then, Emmanuel,' she exclaimed with fresh tears, 'it would have been more loyal in you to have told me that you no longer trusted, that you no longer loved me. I should, perhaps, have been resigned in thinking that I went away from you with your esteem; but to drive me away with your scorn, to accuse me of treachery, to write me that which you have written to me, to make a woman that you professed to love suffer thus—it is horrible, it is horrible; and one day, I hope, you will repent it.'

"'Do not speak of repenting, madame,' I said to her; 'for who shall say whether we ought to repent of not having loved enough, or of having loved too much?'

"'That is still an insult,' said she, sadly, 'is it not? Well, I pardon you for it, as I have pardoned you always; for, indeed, few days have passed since I have known you that you have not flung some insult in my face. You are yet young, Emmanuel, and you know neither the happiness of love nor the luxury of pardon. Later, it will be your lot to love another woman; one who will have, perhaps, a past more sad than mine even has been; it is then, and then only, that you will comprehend the wrong, the injustice, that you do me now; and that thus seeing, you will proffer me your hand, saying, "Yes, you were in the right.'"

"If I had but listened to my heart, I should, whilst

craving from her a pardon, have thrown myself into her arms; but the voice of pride was louder, and I listened to that only; in defiance of my conscience, I sought to convince myself she had deceived me, and I hardened myself in my wickedness. She looked at me, and through her tears I divined the emotions of her heart.

"I profited by my advantage; and said to her—

"'I thank you for your ethics, madame; but I believe them to be as false as your love; and you will permit me the liberty to no longer profit by the one or the other.'

"'You act violently in speaking thus to me, Emmanuel; it must be that some one whom I do not know has irritated you against me. You are good in disposition, I know you are. Often have I seen the tear brim your eyes at the recital of suffering; therefore, I know that something must have blinded you that you do not see what I suffer. Come,' said she, with tenderness, taking my hands, 'come, avow to me that this is but some proof that you have wished to make; say to me that it was only that you wished to be certain of my love, and that you have only written that letter but to test and to judge of my heart by witnessing that which the ordeal would create.'

"'No,' said I, 'do not deceive yourself; cruel as that letter may appear to you, it is but simply the expression of my thoughts; and if to-day it has made you suffer, yesterday it was my lot to suffer.'

"'But you know that I do not deceive you.'

" 'What proof have I?'

" 'All! Come, reason a little, and calmly; sit down near to me; say—tell me, what interest have I to deceive you? Are you my husband, my brother, my son? The links that unite us are but those that the will can loosen and indifference break. If I did not love you, who could have forced me to come here day by day, to bear your anger without reason; your scorn without cause? Well, then, if I come, it must be because I love you; if I come it must be, that even in that scorn I find a charm, and that you are dearer to me with your anger than another with his love; it is, that I see you young, that I believe you good; it is that I would—pardon me this vanity—that you should owe to me some of the happiness of your life; and that, when you no longer love me enough to be my lover, you will love me yet enough to remain my friend. I know well enough to what I expose myself in loving a man of your age; the disdain, the unfaithfulness,' said she, with a smile of love and pardon beaming on her face; 'well, then, if I brave all that—if I humiliate at your feet my reputation, my pride, my heart—there must indeed be reason with me. That reason cannot be one of interest; and it must be therefore one of love.'

" I had nothing to reply to all this. Something said to me that she was right; and yet I heard and listened to a voice that, from the depths of my stupid, perverse vanity cried to me, 'She deceives you, and laughs at you; you are not the first she has loved; does she remember the others?—woman that swears, mouth that lies.

"'Yet,' I began after a silence, 'you know the man whom they say is your lover?'

"'I do.'

"'He comes to your house?'

"'He does.'

"'Often?'

"'Every evening.

"'And wherefore?'

"'He is one of my brother's friends, and every evening my brother dines with us.'

"'And that man is nothing to you?'

"'Nothing save a friend, but a devoted friend.'

"'There is no devotedness with men but when there is love—that man is your lover.'

"'What!—you are going to recommence? Heavens! by what must one swear to make you believe?'

"'Swear not—act!'

"How must I act?'

"'You must not see that man any more.'

"'That is an impossibility.'

"'You see!' said I, all my doubts flooding back upon me.

"'Reflect; it is my brother's friend—one of his companions at college; I myself was yet at school when I first knew him. What excuse can I frame for no longer receiving him; and more, above all, why should I not receive him any more?'

"'Because that man compromises you.'

"'Who says so? who dares to say so?' she asked, the colour mantling to her face.

"'Everybody.'

"'And who believes it?'

"'I DO; and that suffices.'

"'You are a child.'

"'That is possible; but you shall choose between the man and the child, between the lover and the friend.'

"What do you mean by that?'

"'I mean to say that I will never permit a suspicion, even if unjust, where I love. I say that that suspicion, which I cannot contradict without compromising you, becomes a reality, if you do not aid me to destroy it. I say, that however honourable it may be, I accept not the rivalry of anybody; I say in fact, that you must either cease from seeing this man, or you must cease to come to me.'

"Scarcely had I pronounced these words than all palely she arose; I repented of that which I had said, but it was too late. I made a movement to again approach towards her; she drew back, extending her hand to arrest my step.

"'You are wrong, Emmanuel,' she said; 'the word with which a woman is driven away is a word of which he heart repents for ever. Adieu!'

"My head sank upon my breast. There was so much of tears, so much of truth in the tone of that woman's voice, that the terrible knowledge of what I was doing so frightfully overwhelmed me, that could I have spoken, I had not even dared to sue for pardon. I saw, as she opened the door, that she turned once again to me with a look I shall never forget.

"I stood motionless. She believed, doubtless, that it was indifference ; but it was fear, it was terror. I repeat it now, so enormous did my fault appear to me, that it seemed impossible to redeem it.

"When the door closed after her, I still, nevertheless, dared to wish to convince myself, against conscience, that I was securing my happiness, and I cried aloud in my madness—

"'At last I am free!' Yet I sprang to the window, and watched the dark shadow that, on turning the street, gave a last look towards my house."

CHAPTER V.

SUEING FOR PARDON.

"I DRESSED myself and went out; I returned early, and inquired if there was a letter for me. There was not. Would you believe that I was astonished at this?

"The next day the same silence; there was no letter. Then I wrote a letter myself, or rather ten letters, for I knew not what to say. Some were full of excuses, the others were full of reproaches; I did not send any of them.

"On the third day—and this even whilst I did not love this woman—I made to myself pretexts for passing under her windows. I had a friend—no, he was not even a friend, an acquaintance—that I had not seen for a year, and whom I had not the least reason to go and visit, save that he lived in the same quarter as she did; therefore I went.

"The windows before which I wished to pass were all closed. I did not find my friend, or rather my pretext; this delighted me. I returned, of course, by the same route, but for the same result—the windows were closed.

"Two days passed thus. The third day on entering, I received a little packet; there was a purse inside and a letter.

"'If no longer to meet, one must at least acquit one's

self; receive, Emmanuel, this purse, that I had commenced with you and for you, and that I have finished during the last two evenings; it is not a gift, it is a debt; keep it in remembrance of a friend.'

"I replied merely with a cold letter. Going out, I met the individual who had made the assertion before me at the dinner-table at St Mandé, respecting Madame d'Harnebey. I accosted him with an air of indifference, and questioned him anew on the subject. He related the same things to me; and more, on seeing my doubt, said that if I would go that same evening to the opera, I should see that woman there with her husband and her lover. 'They never leave one another,' he added. Then I went to the residence of one of those fallen beings of whom I had already spoken. I asked her if she would come with me that evening to the opera. As you can imagine, she accepted the invitation with eagerness. I knew where Madame d'Harnebey's box was. I went to the office and took the box exactly facing it. At eight o'clock we were in the theatre. At half past eight she arrived with her husband and the friend in question. I confess to you that my heart beat frightfully on seeing the prediction of the morning realized.

"She was beautiful as an angel, but she appeared sad in the midst of her flowers and her beauty. All at once her eyes turned towards the side of the house on which we were sitting; on seeing me with a female, she involuntarily started back.

" Mine was the triumph! I doubt not but that she feigned sudden indisposition, for before the end of the third act, she rose up and went out, and the box was empty.

" From that day forward, for nearly three weeks, I did not hear her spoken of any more. Every day I inquired if there were any letters for me; not a word—no letters came. This oblivion in which she left me, this indifference that she perhaps affected for me, humiliated me, drove me into a fever; and now this woman—whom formerly I fancied I did not love, now that I suspected her of no longer loving me, but of loving another—explain the change as you will—I loved her passionately, but I loved her weeping like a child. I sought for her everywhere; but whether it was that she evaded me, or that she had left Paris, I could meet with her nowhere—I could find her nowhere. At last, one morning, I could no longer bear the suspense. I wrote to her. But I did not dare to ask her to come to me, and I did not dare to go to her house; I therefore asked her to meet me in the garden of the Tuileries. 'Come to-morrow,' I wrote to her, 'at nine o'clock, upon the terrace on the river side; come as if it was the question of life and death to a man.'

" At half-past eight the next day I was on the garden terrace. At nine o'clock she came; she was looking a little thin. She came up to me and offered me her hand.

" 'You have made me very much afraid,' were the first words she spoke to me.

" 'Why?' I said to her.

" 'Your letter was so urgent, that it made me tremble with fear that you were menaced with a great woe.'

" Whilst she was thus speaking to me, she walked in the direction to where two isolated chairs were standing. I followed her mechanically.

" 'Urgent even as was my letter, it could not,' I said, convey to you one tithe of what I suffer.'

" 'You suffer?'

" 'I do.'

" 'And what is it that makes you suffer thus?'

" 'Listen to me. Tell me, since I have not seen you, have you sometimes thought of me?'

" 'Every day; day by day.'

" 'And you have despised me?'

" 'I pitied you.'

" 'Do you believe that even for some of the faults that are committed there can be a repentance that can expiate, and that a pardon can be given?'

" 'I do so believe.'

" 'Even when it is a base insult to a woman?'

" 'You see my belief is that also, since I am here.'

" 'Well, then, you must pardon; and you must forget, above all, the three weeks that are about to end; you must restore to me, were it but a little, of that love that formerly you gave me unbroken, all entire; if you will not, I declare to you I know not what will become of me.'

"A sad smile passed over the lips of Madame d'Harnebey, a smile full of lamentation and regret; but it was without a ray of triumph, spite of her victory.

"'That is impossible,' she said.

"'Impossible!' cried I; 'have you not just told me that all can be pardoned?'

"'But I ought to have added, that we have not the power of forgetting; and on me you have inflicted wounds from which I shall suffer all my life.'

"'What!' I cried, in angu sh—'what is that you tell me?'

"'My friend,' she replied calmly, 'I tell you, that to my first days of silence—silence that was intended as a means to make you reflect, and through that to recall you to me—you replied but by indifference. I had yet more than pardoned you, for at that period I loved you still. To the letter that I wrote to you, and in which every honest-hearted man ought to have recognised love and pardon, you responded with a disgraceful letter, that I tore to pieces with tears. Nevertheless, if you had at that moment asked from me that which you ask to-day, I should have forgotten all, for I loved you then as ever; but, Emmanuel, remember one evening that I was at the opera, not for my pleasure, but that I was compelled to be there, for my refusals to go there had astonished the one who had the best right to be so astonished; one evening—you will remember it—that all in my sadness, with the flowers on my brow, but the tears in my eyes ready to fall, I saw you seated in a box, you, whom I still loved so much—you, braving the public gaze with a woman by your side. You know not all the wrong that you have done me; for a moment's space—terrible moment of transition from love to indifference!—you forced me—forced me to despise you! That which you did there was more than wicked, it was cowardly; although I would have given all the world to have had the strength to bear that which I then witnessed—but you saw that I left. Oh! if you knew how I wept that night! And yet I felt that I loved you still. Then came to me the all-pervading desire to raise between you and myself an insuperable, eternal barrier; for we weak women, we have not, like you, self-reliance and our power in ourselves; we lose our head instantly, and we cling to the first support that meets our grasp, even should that stay burn our hand; then, Emmanuel, then—and therein is that which above all your soul ought to repent, for then—'

"Her voice faltered, and she broke off.

"'Then?' I half whispered, trembling as a leaf to divine, to anticipate, her meaning.

"'Then,' she resumed, 'the words which you have said of me, and which I swear to you upon my honour were false, the day after that evening at the opera were true. You see, Emmanuel, that from day to day you can be no more than a friend for me; but all that friendship can do I will do. When in your turn you love a woman, consult me, and I will tell you what you must do, that she shall love you in return.'

"'You jest with me, madame,' said I with bitterness; 'that is not generous.'

"'Jest with you! Can you entertain such a thought?'

"'And now,' said I, 'you love that man?'

"'Who has told you—I have not—that I love him?'

"'And yet you are his?'

"'I had the conviction that you loved another.'

"'What proved to you that I loved that woman whom I accompanied to the opera?'

"What proved to you that man was my lover? You see, Emmanuel, that I am frank, therefore it is that I repeat to you, that from this moment there can be nought save friendship between us; friendship enduring and sincere will it be on my part. You have a hundred times pointed out my past existence to me as a cause for remorse; I have ever pardoned your so doing. Remember! —mark me, I say it without reproach, for now we have nothing to reproach one another with—remember how cruel you have been to me; remember how many times you have cast that stone which none—it has Divine forbiddance—dares to cast on the transgressor. I had entirely pardoned you, for even among your offences I could not conjecture jealousy; but I again repeat to you, that night at the opera rent asunder the last links that could attach me to you, and the day following shattered the last links that could attach you to me; so then, Emmanuel, let us each retake our former existence. It is you that have desired that this should be. Become, on your part, an indifferent man once again; myself,' she added, with a smile of terrible bitterness, 'a thoughtless woman; but bear away with you from this conversation —perhaps the last that we shall have together—the eternal conviction that I have never loved but you. Now, adieu! and if ever it is yours to suffer, and you want a friend, remember me.'

"She held out her hand to me, which I touched mechanically, and without adding a word she passed down the long green vista of the avenue, and disappeared."

CHAPTER VI.

SHE CAME—SHE IS GONE!

"I WAS annihilated. I returned home raving with fever. How I loved that woman! I wrote letters of madness to her; I cast myself at her feet; I proffered myself the minion to her word; I immolated my self-pride before her will; to her wish I would be her slave. She replied to me with cold yet gentle letters, detailing, with that lucidity which indifference gives, the impossibility of a renewed attachment.

"Wherever I knew that I could meet Henriette I went. I wrote to her every evening how I spent my life each day; she replied to me; she also gave me appointments to meet her. I saw her one hour, two hours; and then I was a week without seeing her. In the end, that passion which I had for her made such progress, and her firmness in not listening to me was so real, that I fell ill. I wrote to her to come and see me; she wrote back to me, but at first she did not come, fearing that I was setting a snare for her. At length, however, she came—came as my friend; nursing me like a mother, consoling me as a sister.

"Ultimately I recovered; but the shock had been so violent that the doctor ordered me to go to the south. At the risk of compromising herself she accompanied me as far as the carriage, and she promised to write to me. I started for Italy.

"In the first letter that I wrote to her I implored her to write back to me the one word that should bid my return. She replied, but the one word was not in it.

"I became reckless, heartless. I went so far as to fancy at Naples that I had become in love with a *danseuse.* I returned to Paris with her, and as I knew where Madame d'Harnebey walked every day, I endeavoured to promenade with my new mistress in the same places and at the same hours. The first time I met her she saluted me with her hand, and without the least emotion.

"For some time I no longer heard her spoken of; but still I held her always in my heart, and one day entered her house, and made inquiries about her. They replied to me that, having lost her little girl, she had retired into the country. About eight days after that I saw her pass by me dressed in mourning. She made a sign to me with her hand, and I have never seen her more."

Pausing from his recital, Emmanuel quaffed a brimming glass of champagne, as if it had been the water of Lethe; then he arose, and offering his hand—

"Now I must go home," said he. "May we meet again soon!" and he went away—I could almost have said that he escaped.

AUGUSTINE, THE GRISETTE.

THE GRISETTE.

CHAPTER I.

MYSTERIES.

IT was some days after the evening of the masked ball, that I was loitering on the Boulevards, whiling away one of those beautiful days of winter, when the sun appears proportionately the more benignant as he is rare, when, on turning my head to look after a pair of pretty feet, which you know I so admire, I ran against another promenader, whose visual organs had also deviated at that moment from the right line, probably from a similar cause. Recovering the collision, I found it was Emmanuel; we burst into hearty laughter, and I gave him my hand.

"By Jove!" said I to him, "this meeting is most opportune; I dream over the experiences you confided to me, and am always regretting not having my complete number."

"What number?"

"The number of stories I am to have."

"What! after all that I have related you are not content?"

"No," replied I; "no more content than is a hungry man, to whom it is said, after the first plate at a well-served table, 'Now get up and go.'"

"Well, that's very flattering, but I have not the time now to relate anything else to you. I am left to a mere incident, of which I make almost a romance, and I fancy it will be all but devoid of interest after that which you heard the other evening."

"Then tell me in four words what it is."

"You want it, then?"

"Well, then, yes, I do want it."

"Ah! wretched man, you are going to sell my woes and my souvenirs by the page."

"Exactly so."

"You have devoted yourself, then, to the career of letters?" said Emmanuel, jocularly.

"Yes, I have."

"Well, then, why don't you invent?"

"One does not invent, you know; we relate.'

"Well, I have already given you two histories, to which you must have the counterpart?"

"Just so."

"It is as though you had the two sides of a triangle; the third is not difficult to find."

"It is not the sentiment that I seek for, but the details of the story. The type I have; and I am sure you have the illustrat ve incidents, and it is these that I want."

"Explain yourself," said Emmanuel.

"Why this is what I mean; Madame d'Harnebey is a type of the woman whose love leaves the trace of its passages in the heart; this love is a passion."

"Well?"

"Antonia, whom you now know: the love of her is what I shall designate as a folly, which leaves but few traces, save in the pocket; it is the genuine love-affair of pleasure; of Paris-life the custom."

"Very well."

"Now, to make your life complete, you ought to have known the love of another *genre* of woman."

"I'm listening; explain."

"There is missing, to complete, the love of the woman who has been seen but once, who is perhaps never seen afterwards, who leaves no souvenir, save perhaps in the memory; and this love I shall call a caprice. Such a woman is loved for a period of two days. If by chance she is met again her hand is clasped with pleasure, and you are nearly loving her once more, for she has neither ruined your mind, nor your heart, nor your fortune. This phase of love is but a delightful dream that has had a form; it is an ideal that has had a body for the space of five minutes; if I believe in my presentiments, the woman to whom I saw you speaking at the ball is one of this kind."

"That is true."

"Well, then, let us go into the club, light our cigars, and you relate me your adventures with her."

"But listen to me," said Emmanuel, pausing, and leaning on the balustrade of the stairs of the club when we entered; "I am willing to tell you all, but on one condition."

"Name it."

"It is, that if you publish this history you will change all the names."

"Certainly, that's understood."

"But, stay, that is not all either; you must wait until such moment that I authorise you to give it to the public."

"And why all these mysteries?"

"Because this adventure, though without the least importance in my life, may be of great importance in the life of her who is its heroine."

We were in the saloon of the club, which at that hour was quite deserted; we threw ourselves on the divan, and after having lighted our cigars and settled ourselves comfortably, Emmanuel to relate, and I to listen, I turned to him, and, with mock solemnity, said—

"I accept the conditions; speak, I hearken to thee."

CHAPTER II.

AN EXCITING SCENE.

"I TOLD you," commenced Emmanuel, "that I had taken possession of a modest suit of rooms in the Rue Neuve des Mathurius. I do not think that I gave you any other particulars."

"None; some recollection in the history of Madame d'Harnebey seized you, and called your attention from the subject."

"Well, then, I was very sad indeed when I took possession of those rooms. I was getting really ill, and fancied myself becoming misanthropic. I broke away from the society of all women; I would no longer hear them spoken about. Contrary to the habit of all young men of my class, I returned home to my rooms at a very early hour every evening. I read; and when my porter —(for at that period I did not allow myself any other domestic)—when my porter came in the morning to light my fire I never chatted with him, nor made inquiries of the other people in the house; this may the more have astonished the honest fellow, as often, when in the evening I took my waxlight from his room at the entrance of the house, I saw in his lodge a tenant, and a very pretty tenant, and one living on the same floor as myself.

"For all my resolution to live the life of a hermit, I had not failed to remark the neighbour, for at the age I then was, though we fancy the heart consumed, yet the sight of a pretty face will re-illume the flame altogether. I often, as I have already told you, met the damsel when I have entered in the evening. Our staircase was exceedingly narrow. It followed, therefore, that she went first, and ascended slowly, with the step of one who knows that there are five flights of stairs to mount. I who came after, saw a neatly-shod foot, a slender leg. I know not if you are of my taste, but I am an admirer of a little foot, a leg, though slender, yet promising not to continue so, and, above all, a spotless white stocking, which loses itself in a well-made boot. My neighbour had these attractions. Now, mentally strengthened by my resolutions, I sometimes ventured to say to her after the first flight—'Pardon me, mademoiselle:' implying, 'Will you allow me to pass?' and then, raising my hat to her, I preceded her, and scaled my four last flights and entered my room. While I was fastening my door I could hear her arrive at hers, open it, shut it—and thus it ended.

"But there were some days that I did not pass before my neighbour, in which the contemplation of these two little feet, disappearing each in theit turn to the step above, to reappear with a silken patter, absorbed me; and, arrived at our fifth floor, we found ourselves opening our doors together and shutting them at the same time. This coincidence occasioned me, without thinking, to cast a glance at her rooms, which could be seen from her door. I could discern a very comfortable interior, but with nothing that suggested an outlay beyond her modest position in society.

"Since I have very rapidly, yet none the less completely, expressed my impression of her apartments, I owe you the analysis of her face. She was pale and thin, but I do not think this any disparagement. Let me make a comparison, though perhaps a little fantastic—she suggested to me those thin taper bottles of Rhine wine, which contain such an excellent liquor, whilst those stone clumsy bottles called *litres*, solid on their bases, ample in outline, insolent in appearance, contain such excellent wine.

"You have asked me for my second history, so I give it to you with all my impressions in detail; and you will want these details when you write it, for indeed it is the history of a caprice and not of a passion."

"I very well like," continued Emmanuel, "the style of woman we have now under review. I am not one of those blockheads who say—this one, 'I like only dark women;' the other one, 'I like only fair women;' for myself, I do not fall in love, but I am nearly loving them all. You can understand, then, that for all others than myself, my neighbour would have been a treasure; unhappily, I had made a vow, and could not swerve from it; then, were I even captivated by her, nothing had discovered that she cared anything about me ; and I did not fancy that I had the resolution to make love for a long time to a woman with no feeling for me. She had pretty teeth, lips bright as blood ; this proved that my neighbour was thin by nature ; her eyes were black, her nose straight, her air *distingue*. It was the winter season ; she sometimes wore a little felt bonnet, sometimes a bonnet of black velvet, a cape of dark cloth, a dress of brown silk, and a muff. She seemed to have all that was necessary to be well and comfortably dressed, and with nothing to occasion a remark ; she wore no jewellery. There—that is all that I saw, and all that I knew. Full of the recollections that came to me of Madame d'Harnebey, I thought not of my neighbour, save when I met her ; but this meeting was such a regular habit each evening, that I was half astonished when I did not chance to see her ; and I involuntarily cast a glance at her door in passing before I entered my own. In the meantime my misanthropy shortened its duration, and, by degrees, I began once more to frequent the society of my old comrades ; who, seeing me no longer in love, did not counsel me any more, and helped to divert me from my recollections. Sometimes I went to supper with them ; sometimes they came to supper with me. It is useless to bring many together at supper if there is not to be any laughing, therefore we laughed. My friends—(since this word must always be returned to)—my friends, who had no reason for being sad, sung, shouted, and created disturbance to such a pitch that I was sometimes forced—being a very modest tenant, and reputed quiet until then—to give them notice to quit, that the proprietor should not give me notice. At last I began to be quite unsettled. Friendship had recovered its rights; as for love it was set on one side. The result of all this was, that sometimes I entered very late, and that I more rarely saw my neighbour; but, from time to time, my friends had met her on the stairs in coming to my apartment.

"'Who is that girl that lives on the same floor as you?" they asked.'

"'I don't know at all,' was my answer.

"'What! you don't know at all?'

"'I know her by sight, that is all.'

"'Well, that is good! You have in your house, and on the same floor, a charming woman, and you don't make her acquaintance!"

"'For what end or object?'

"'For what do they make the acquaintance of young and pretty women? And a woman that you have under your hand, as well?'

"'It is exactly because I have her under my hand that I do not wish to know her,' replied I.

"'Will you give us your reason?'

"'If I make her acquaintance, I shall make love to her. There are only two results to this; that she refuses me, or that she accepts me.'

" 'Naturally.'

" 'If she refuses me, then I am in the stupid position of a neighbour who is not received, and who is laughed at; if she accepts me, it is still worse.'

" 'How so?'

" 'From the day that I am her lover, she, being my neighbour, will be always with me or I with her. It follows that, for the sake of peace, I shall be forced to no longer receive those of my friends who do not please her. Then, the day that we may differ, I should be compelled, so as to avoid the scenes women create, to quit my lodgings; and, if one thing more than another influences me, it is that; for nothing bores me like changing my lodgings.'

" 'That's true; but these reasons, excellent for you, do not exist for us; and we have, thanks to you, the means of attainment, without having the result to fear.'

" 'As you like; but I doubt if you will succeed, for that little girl appears very quiet; and, after the noise that you make here, she must be convinced that you are not of the same character as herself.'

"The feeling which influenced me in thus speaking is strange, nevertheless natural. I did not know that woman; I did not love her; and yet it was disagreeable to me to think that one of my friends might become her lover; and, if I had perceived that either one of them had the serious intention of endeavouring to become so, I believe I should have commenced the campai the campaign the next day, for the purpose of outstripping him. Author, explain that," said Emmanuel, smiling.

"That is very easy; continue."

"As I have told you, it sometimes occurred that I entered at a rather advanced hour of the night. The lamps on the stairs were extinguished; Father Jean, my porter, was asleep; I did not wish to wake him up, therefore I mounted without a light, and groped my way with my hands. One night, at the moment that I gained the last stair of my fifth flight, I made a false footing, and stumbled three or four steps. You know when you fall on the stairs what a row it makes? I had just recovered, when I heard my neighbour's door open, and I saw her appear with a light in her hand.

"'You have hurt yourself, sir?' she said. And, through the interest she appeared to show for me, I discerned that smile which has always birth, especially on the lips of a female, at the sight of any one surprised in a ridiculous position. I thanked her, in rising up.

"'You have no light, then?' replied she.

"'No,' I responded, smiling too, at the idea of the situation in which our acquaintance was commencing.

"'Well, then, take this candle, sir; you will only be tumbling again!' And I saw that she was making efforts to prevent herself from laughing outright.

"'That is needless, madame; if you will permit me, I will light only this paper.' At the same time I pulled from my pocket a paper, which I twisted up and lighted;

then I bowed to my neighbour, who returned me a gracious inclination of the head, and retired into her room. Whilst I held my torch with my left hand, and with the other hand put the key into the lock, it seemed to me that there was talking in the lady's apartment; I listened, and heard her say—'It is the gentleman on the same floor, who has tumbled on the stairs;' a phrase that was followed by two laughs, executed by a soprano voice and a baritone voice. This was the first time that I had perceived the presence of a man with my neighbour. It must have been two o'clock in the morning. I got into my bed, saying, 'Oh! oh!' I took a book and commenced reading, but by degrees my head fell back; my hand abandoned the book, and my thoughts turned to Madame d'Harnebey. I left an evening party of young men, I had come from a great noise, and I found myself in the midst of a deep calm. I asked myself what, at that hour, that woman could be doing, whom I had rendered so unhappy, and who had made me so sad. Whilst I was thus dreaming, I heard my neighbour's door open, and shut almost immediately. 'That is doubtless the baritone voice that is leaving,' thought I. Then the silence and my thoughts retook their course. I could not then find anything better to give a form to my remembrances than to read over again the last letter of Madame d'Harnebey, which was in the pocket of my coat. But I searched in vain everywhere; the letter was lost. I naturally thought it had fallen on the stairs at the moment of my drawing out the paper to take a light; so, putting on my slippers and my trousers, I went out, the candle in my hand, to search on the stairs; but I found nothing near the place where I had tumbled. I thought then that the letter had, perhaps, flown over the rail of the baluster, and I went down the five flights, searching step by step, but, nevertheless, fruitlessly—it was not there. I remounted quite baffled, for the letter, fallen from my pocket, and yet in its envelope, could only have been lost where I had taken my coat off, or where I had opened the pocket to take out something. It could only then have been found by my friends, or by that gentleman who had left my neighbour. Then, beyond the pain that I had in losing the letter, I felt greatly annoyed by the chance that it should have been found by one of those fellows I had been with that evening.

"You know what the letter of the woman you love is, who believes that that which she writes will only be read by yourself?—it is full of words understood by each of you, and which each of you find charming, but which appear supremely ridiculous to the indifferent person who reads the letter by accident; especially when the indifferent person has in his pocket one of his own love-letters, like the one he has found; for all love-letters resemble one another, or must do so a little.

"When the name of that one to whom such a letter is addressed is not on the envelope, it matters little, and still more it matters little to him who has found it. But when that loser knows that it will be recognised to be one that he has inspired; wben he knows that in the eyes of those who know him, and who ask for nothing better for a laugh, he is going to have that improbable and stupid position of a *man beloved*, he becomes furious at having dropped such a letter; he remembers the expressions that were in it, and he sees himself that he would have been very ready to have been amused with such a letter had he found it, addressed to anybody instead of himself. In my case it was yet still worse. It was not an ordinary love-letter; this was one of those letters which shelter the last remembrances of a love-affair that is broken asunder, the last regrets of a love that is shattered; one of those letters in which the heart of a woman overflows, and which resemble precious and fragile roses, full of incense and perfumes, which fall to pieces in the hands of unskilled beings who touch them.

"I had nearly the tears in my eyes in thinking that the love of that woman, the grief of which I was the cause, that all those impressions, in short, which she had so ingenuously confided to the letter that I had lost, were about to be burlesqued by a parcel of fools incapable of understanding them, or by my neighbour and her lover, who would make no scruple in looking at it. My searches did not, however, lead to any discovery, and my reflections did not afford me any consolation.

"I had re-entered my room in despair, and had shut my door, when I saw a paper lying on the ground. I stooped down, I picked it up; it was my letter in an envelope. I had lost it, so it appeared, at my door, and, in going out precipitately to seek for it, I had passed by it without seeing it. I hastened at once to my bed, and began to open it; but when I went to draw it from the envelope, I found an obstacle, and I then perceived that, since I had lost it, the envelope had been resealed. For a moment I thought I was dreaming. I rubbed my eyes, and looked attentively at the seal. In the place of the black wax which had originally fastened the envelope, there had been put red wax, and instead of the initial that there was on the first seal, I found on this second one an A. 'Is that the initial of my neighbour, or of her lover?' I asked of myself. In the first case it might be a lover's jest; in the second case, it might be an impertinence; but an impertinence of which a man well brought up would be incapable, and she would only receive a well-bred man. On the contrary, thought I, she has seen the letter tumble from my pocket, and, wanting to gratify her curiosity, she has not warned me of it; then she came to seek it when she saw me go in, and she has wished to read it with that gentleman, who has not consented to this, and he has told her to slide it under my door. But then, why has she replaced the original seal by her own? It would have been better to have gut the letter as it was under my door; I should then have believed that I lost in my room, and not outside, and I should not have suspected that they had been able to read it, whilst now I was at the least sure that she had. But however it may be, I urged to myself, I have my letter, and if they can say that I am ridiculous, at least they can't prove it. Now, if my neighbour had written to me, and had put her letter under the same envelope as that of the other, the second seal would have been not only excusable but necessary. I broke open the seal, but I found only my letter, without their having added a word. As I read my letter over again, with heart full of divers sentiments, I seemed to see on the other side of the page the bantering head of my neighbour. At last I went to sleep, without having unravelled the occurrence, but with full decision to have the details on the first opportunity, and at the first sign of the knowledge of that letter which should betray who had found it.

"The next day I was yet asleep, when Father Jean entered my chamber. I did not open my eyes, but I said—

"'Father Jean, how do they call that gentleman who came to my neighbour's yesterday evening?'

"'Frederic, sir,' replied the porter.

"'And his other name?'

"'We only know him under the name of Frederic, sir.'

"'And my neighbour—her name?'

"'Augustine.'

"'Augustine? just so,' said I; 'that's all right.'

"'What do you say, sir?'

" 'Nothing, thank you.'

" 'That's a very nice little woman, that Mademoiselle Augustine,' continued Father Jean.

" Unhappily I had not the intention to question my porter; therefore I cut short the information that I saw he was ready to give me, by saying to him, 'Give me my boots,' and I rose and went out.

" In going down I met Augustine, whom I saluted with a bow. She responded to me with a very amiable 'Good-day, sir,' and I saw that she waited for me to interrogate her about the letter, just as I waited for her to be the first to speak of it.

" Neither one nor the other dared to venture on the subject. She lingered a minute with Father Jean; I passed on, saluting her a second time as I went by.

" I met her again without any other converse than the 'Good-day, sir,' 'Good-day, mademoiselle,' that we exchanged in most amicable tone. In the meantime the manner of that woman evidenced a certain curiosity in me, which recurred to my mind from time to time; and it is doubtless through this that it finished by Augustine occupying a corner in my thoughts.

" You know that one fine day, wearied with the life that brought me no consolation, I resolved to leave for Italy? I said, therefore, to Father Jean, that I was about to leave in five or six days, and that he must have everything ready for my departure. The day following the one on which I had communicated my project to

Father Jean, there came a rap at my door. It was about mid-day. I went and opened the door—it was Augustine.

" 'Pardon me, sir,' she said to me; 'I am disturbing you?'

" 'No, not at all.'

" 'Have you a fire in your room?'

" 'Oh yes.'

" 'Will you, then, let me warm myself a little? The bricklayers are at my fireplace, and I am freezing.'

" 'Pray come in,' I said.

" It was a visit the ostensible motive for which was original enough, and certainly it was unexpected enough. I introduced my visitor to my little saloon, which was rather elegantly furnished.

" 'Ah!' said she, looking at the mantel-piece ornaments, 'what charming Saxony ware you have!'

" 'They are all, or any of them, offered to your acceptance,' I said to her, 'if they please you.'

" 'I did not admire them that they should be offered to me; I should wish to advise you of this, that you may not fear my visits.'

" 'And on my part,' said I to her, 'I never offer anticipating a refusal. To-day, therefore, you break through your usual custom, and accept; and for the future I will leave off mine by not offering any more.'

" Augustine leaned forward gracefully to take from the mantel-piece some little figure she had admired; but after an attentive consideration, she replaced it carefully, and sat down on the hearth-rug before the fire. I thought it seemed more agreeable to her to be thus than in an easy-chair; nevertheless, I offered her one.

"'No,' said she, 'thank you, I like this better.' So I sat down in the easy-chair myself. She raised her large eyes, bright and clear, towards me; you might have compared it to the gaze of a gazelle.

"'You are rather astonished,' she said, 'that I have come thus boldly to see you?'

"'I am enchanted,' was my reply.

"'And why so?'

"'Why? Because it is always agreeable to receive the visit of a charming woman.'

"'You have not long thought in that way.'

"'It is my turn to question,' said I. 'I shall ask you, why have I not?'

"'Because, had you desired to make my acquaintance you would have endeavoured to do so.'

"'I was not sure that my visits would be accepted.'

"'Visits are always accepted when they are made by a well-bred man.' The tone in which she gave these little lessons was delightful.

"'Again, it was necessary that I should be presented,' replied I.

"'You were my neighbour, and with that title you could present yourself. Besides, you meet me every day; I had not a very terrible air; you knew that I had a lover; you could, therefore, rest satisfied that there was no need to put yourself about on my account.' It was evident that she waited my response, to judge me.

" 'At first I was ignorant that you had a lover, mademoiselle. I never made inquiries from any person, and nobody has come to tell me so. When, however, I knew it, you were to me none the less worthy of all the respect that is due to your sex.'

" 'Well,' said she, offering her small, delicate hand, 'you are a charming man, and you shall be my friend.'

" 'Your very devoted friend,' said I.

" 'But now let us talk seriously,' said Augustine.

" 'For my part, all that I shall say will be serious,' I observed, resolved that I would not be taken in fault.

" 'Well, well,' replied she, smiling, " that's settled, say no more; now to speak of other matters—I am told that you are leaving; is it true?'

" 'Yes; I am going.'

" 'And when?'

" 'In six days.'

" 'Really?'

" 'Really.'

" 'And there is no one able to make you remain?' she inquired, looking at me from the corner of her eye.

" 'Yes—you!'

" 'Now don't speak idle words.'

" 'They are not idle; I don't lie; tell me to remain, and I will remain.'

" 'But how can I bid you remain?'

"'In the best way that you can.'

"'Well, it is not for me to bid you.'

"'Command me, then.'

"'I have not the right.'

"'You can take it.'

"'How—I can take it?'

"'As you have taken it with——'

"'With whom?' interrupted she, looking in my face.

"'With others,' replied I, carelessly.

"'With another, you should have said,' was her answer; 'do you fancy that it is with the idea of having you for a lover that I have come to see you? If you do, you deceive yourself, and are a conceited fellow.'

"'Oh! I have not thought so for a minute,' I stammered out, a little intimidated by her clear responses.

"'I said to you just now,' she continued, "'You shall be my friend;" had I intended anything else, I should at once have said, "Be my lover." Now let us return to what I was saying to you: you are going?'

"'Yes.'

"'And nothing detains you?'

"'Nothing.'

"'That is droll! I should have thought that you loved some one.'

"'Nobody.'

"'Ah!' That *Ah!* seemed to say clearly—

"'But how do you match that reply with the letter

that I found?' Yet I was decided not to be the first to speak of that incident. She added, after a pause—

"'That is true; you receive nobody.'

"'Who has told you so?'

"'Father Jean.'

"'You have asked him, then?'

"'Yes.'

"'Can you tell me what interest you have to know that?'

"'It is very simple; since you would not come to me, and I wished to come to you, I made sure beforehand, that I might not disturb you, or vex anybody else, in visiting you. A visit, perhaps, so wrongly interpreted!'

"'That is true; one is no longer discreetly indiscreet.'

"'Discretion?—that is my great virtue.'

"'Oh!'

"'You say?"

"'I say, oh!'

"'And what does that exclamation signify?'

"'It signifies that you are a remarkable exception; for discretion is not the predominating virtue with women.'

"'It is my only one.'

"'And you have never sinned against it?'

"'Never!'

"'Quite sure?'

"'Will you have a proof?'

"'Give it.'

" 'Well, then, the other night in lighting your paper at my candle, you let fall a letter.'

" 'Yes, I did.'

" 'I saw it fall.'

" 'Why did you not tell me that it had fallen?' Augustine bit her lips.

" 'I should have told you, but the thought did not come to me to do so; and, besides, there is no virtue but where there is a struggle.'

" 'There was a struggle, then?'

" 'Certainly; for a moment I desired to know the contents of that letter.'

" 'At that moment, then, there was sin.'

" 'Yes; but you will see that its end was not accomplished; it did not triumph. When you had entered your room again, I went out and picked up the letter. I saw that it was a woman's handwriting; and I drew the letter from the envelope.'

" 'The devil!' said I.

" 'But I immediately returned it, without reading it.'

" 'You'll swear you did?'

" 'Yes, I will.'

" 'Will you lay me a wager of it?'

" She began to laugh; and, avoiding my challenge, said—

" 'It was, perhaps, only that I was wishing to know you that caused me to seal it up again, with my initial. I slipped it under the door, hoping that, when you saw by the seal to whom you were indebted for the restitution of that letter, you would have come, were it only for politeness' sake, to make a visit to the person who had restored it to you.'

" 'I could not recognise the initial,' was my answer; 'I did not know your name; and it could very well have been any other lodger of the house, save you.'

" 'There is something in what you say. To be candid, having heard that you were leaving so soon, I have wished to pray you, in the name of her who writes to you, to remain.'

" 'Since I am leaving, I may tell you, that she is the only one that cannot keep me; true it is, that in this instance she wants an auxiliary, and there cannot be found a more charming one than yourself. You desire that I should stay?'

" 'Yes.'

" 'Why?'

" 'Because he is going.'

" 'Who—who's he

" 'Frederic.'

" 'Oh!—well; but it would be very much more simple to employ your influence to retain him rather than me.

" 'Ah! but, unhappily, though I have for two years had the right to demand, I am now no longer able to entreat.'

" 'He is not very grateful, then. But did I remain by your wish, to what would it lead?'

" 'At first to your not going; for the very departure, when it is made alone, is always repented of at the first halting-place you come to. Then, afterwards, you continue your journey, for you will never confess to being beaten; and, from conceited obstinacy, you say you are amused. If you go, I shall mope myself to death; whilst, if you remain, you will come and visit me, and I shall come and visit you; and we shall pass some nice evenings together.'

" 'Up to what hour?'

" 'Until daylight, if you like.'

" 'You have no friend, then?'

" 'None; he did not wish me to have any.'

" 'If he learns that we visit?'

" 'He will never know it; who will tell him? He is absent. You are my neighbour; we go, we come; no ill-natured suspicion is excited. He has forbidden my receiving any one; I can obey him; I will receive nobody. I will come to you.'

" 'But these facilities for our visiting one another will create other ideas,' said I, in a tone that perfectly construed my phrase.

" 'Those ideas will not come.'

" 'But if they came?'

" 'You will drive them away.'

" 'But, if I cannot drive them away?'

" 'You will triumph, like me, over all indiscretion.'

" 'But if I cannot triumph over it?'

" 'Then I shall put you out at the door, and we shall not see one another any longer, save as we have done hitherto.'

" 'And when he returns?'

" You will cease to come.'

" 'I shall go; I am decided—I shall go.'

" 'Go,' said she; 'but I tell you I shall mope when both of you are away.'

" 'Well, now, I have listened to you for an hour, and the deuce take me if I understand you. Are you a woman? Tell me?'

" 'Certainly I am.'

" 'And how would you have me live with your intimacy without wishing to be your lover?'

" 'I can live well enough with yours without wishing you to be my lover.'

" 'What a beautiful reason! You have a lover; and I—I am alone.'

" 'Go, then,' said she, rising; 'it were better you go; but until you leave, come and see me.'

" 'When does he leave?'

" 'He went yesterday.'

" 'When are you to be found?'

" 'When you like.—You are of a very merry disposition, are you not?' said Augustine, suddenly.

" 'When what I ask for is not denied me,' said I.

" 'But when you have nothing to ask for?'

" 'Well, I am merry even then.'

" 'Yes, so I was thinking; for I hear laughing and singing in your rooms every day; remember from this moment I count upon you to amuse me. Adieu; I declare to you I am disconsolate when I think that you are going away.' And thus speaking, Augus ine had retaken the piece of Saxony ware, and examined it.

" I was again about to urge her to receive my addresses for, spite of all she had said, I was quite puzzled to interpret the girl; but were it that she divined my thoughts, or that her own fancies had the unsettledness she seemed to affect, she said, turning to me—

" 'This is the old Saxony ware, is it not?'

" 'Yes, indeed it is,' was my reply.

" 'It is really adorable,' was her exclamation. 'I thank you; yes, a thousand times I thank you for it. Adieu, neighbour.'

" 'Let's see,' said I to her, squeezing her hand; 'when shall I see you again?'

" 'When I have the desire to see you again I will come and rap; if you are at home you will open; if you are not, I shall go back again and work.'

" You work, then?'

" 'Yes,' she said, 'I work at home, and in a shop. I must go,' she added, presenting her forehead; 'kiss me, and let us be good friends.'

" I kissed her forehead, she opened the door; then, having looked to see if any one was coming up, she ran into her room."

CHAPTER III.

A LETTER OF CONFESSION.

"THE strange girl!" I exclaimed, half audibly, and waving my hand after her, as she closed the door; and I began to falter in my intention of leaving, so was my curiosity excited to see how far I could carry the adventure, so original did it appear. Nevertheless, Augustine did not efface Madame d'Harnebey from my recollection; for, I argued to myself, my neighbour, after all, could only be a coquette, who wished to set me down for her own amusement; or, being without a lover, was seeking to divert herself.

"I was, however, wise enough to observe to myself, that it was not worth while to renounce, for this adventure, a journey that I had promised to myself for a long time past; so I went to the diligence office, to take my place for Chalons. I found the opportunity of immediately exercising my resolution of prompt departure; for there was a vacant place in the *coupe* of the diligence for the third day from then, and I secured it. I had but little time to make my preparations; so I went and dined quietly, and returned home at seven o'clock. At eight o clock there was a rap at the door; it was Augustine.

"'Well,' said I, as she entered, 'I leave on Thursday.'

"It was Tuesday when this took place.

"'Ah!' was her rejoinder; 'positively?'

"'Positively. Here is my ticket from the diligence office.' She took it, and read it.

"'I hope you'll amuse yourself,' she said; then lapsing into silence, she became quite grave. I could scarcely comprehend it; if, at that moment, she had said to me "Remain," without even any promises, without encouragement, even without leaving me to hope, I should have remained. But she did not speak the word, but, after a while, broke the silence by inquiring—

"'You are going to pack your trunk?'

"'Yes.'

"'Shall I help you?'

"'That is the very thing that I want you to do.'

"'I will arrange your linen, then; men don't know how to pack a trunk.'

"'I am myself one of those who pack their trunks two days in advance; at once to have the time, and also to make sure that nothing is forgotten.'

"She went to my chest of drawers, and opened one of them. It was the very one in which were Madame d'Harnebey'? letters. I saw it, and involuntarily made a movement; she saw my movement, and she recognised the writing.

"'Oh! keep yourself quiet,' she said to me; 'I shall no more read them than I have read the other.'

"'Are you mad,' I said to her, 'to talk in that way

to me?' and saying this, I took her head in my two hands, and kissed her on the forehead.

"In her turn she kissed me, and said to me, with a little tone of chagrin—

"'Now, why do you leave?'

"I looked at her; she was really charming. She went to another drawer to take linen out; she bent down bareheaded; I saw her profusion of hair elegantly folded; I saw the outline of a neck well delineated, and always those two little feet, that in their slippers of gilt kid appeared to me yet more tiny. I turned my eyes away.

"'Well, after all, we ought to be very much amused,' she said, with a sigh, 'with what we are doing.' And she carried some shirts from the chest of drawers to the trunk.

"'But since you need not go before six days, why are you leaving in two?'

"'It is you that are the cause.'

"'I that am the cause—how so?'

"'Why, assuredly, in six days I should be in love with you, and then I should not go at all. Well, now, definitely, do you wish me to remain?'

"'Always, on the same conditions?'

"'Yes.'

"'You know well enough that that cannot be, therefore do not speak of it more, or I shall at once leave you and go to my room.'

"She remained with me until midnight, when she left,

promising to return next day. The next day she came. The same chat, the same result. Only I was positively becoming in love, on my word of honour; but I must confess, it was a high-hearted love, that would, perhaps, have disappeared when its end was won. Meanwhile the idea possessed me that she was making fun of me, and I felt that I must have my heart free from such doubt.

"'Listen,' said I to her; 'I dine this evening with my mother. I shall return, but late; I leave at an early hour to-morrow, and I should not like to leave without seeing you; therefore, I will leave the key in the door, for I may, perhaps, fall asleep by the fire; come at such hour as you like, and wake me up if I sleep.'

"'You can go to bed if you like,' was her reply.

"'This evening, then?' said I.

"'This evening.'

"I returned home at eleven o'clock; I went to bed, and I fell asleep. I must have been some time asleep, when I was aroused, fancying I heard a noise; I woke up, and I saw Augustine, who, seated in an easy chair, was stirring the fire with one hand, and holding a book with the other.

"At this moment it struck one o'clock.

"'You have been there a long time,' I said to her.

"'Since midnight,' was her reply.

"'And what are you doing?'

"'I am reading.'

"'Why have you not woke me up?'

" 'You slept so well, I thought that you wanted repose; and so that I am not alone, is all that I care for; you know that; and I should have passed the night thus.'

" 'Come and sit a little on my bed,' I said to her.

" She put her book away, and came and sat by the side of me. This seemed to me an unheard-of confidence, if it was not somewhat gay and saucy, and I could not reconcile it with her previous protests; the lover came back to my heart again, and I said, taking her hands—

" 'Come, Augustine, do you really love Frederic?'

" 'Yes,' was her answer; but I thought I detected a carelessness in her tone.

" 'And you will not leave him?'

" 'No.'

" 'Nor deceive him?'

" 'No.'

" 'But since it is not a serious love between you?'

" 'It is a sincere love,' she replied; 'I have promised not to deceive him, and I will not.'

" 'But,' continued I, passing my hand round her waist, and drawing her gently towards me, 'but if you love another?'

" 'I love no one,' replied she, endeavouring calmly and without affectation to disengage herself.

" 'I hurt you?' inquired I.

" 'No,' she responded, 'but I prefer sitting down.'

" As though not heeding her wish I still detained her.

" ' Why do you wish to sit down? you do not fear me, surely?'

" ' No; but I inconvenience you.'

" ' Not in the least;' and I still endeavoured to detain her, and in my earnestness, with what, though unintentionally on my part, might have been thought rudeness. Then she broke away from my arm, and started up with so rapid a movement as to escape me, but she did not utter a syllable; she went before the mirror and adjusted her dress, and having relighted her candle, she said to me coldly, ' Adieu!'

" ' Come now,' exclaimed I, holding out my hand to her, ' are you going?'

" ' Yes.' She looked at me, pale and dejected.

" ' Yes,' she continued, ' because were I to remain longer, for you to renew your rudeness, I should quit you with the certainty that you were a man without a mind, and one in whom I could have no belief. Adieu!'

" ' Your hand,' said I. She hesitated.

" ' You need not fear; I am full of regrets. I will not forget myself again.'

" I took her hand—that hand was burning. That girl, perhaps, has no heart, I said to myself, but she has senses.

" ' At what hour do you leave?' she inquired.

" ' At eleven o'clock.'

" ' At ten I will come to bid you adieu. Good night.'

"'Good night. You pardon me?'

"'It must be done, since you are leaving.'

"She went on, shutting all the doors behind her. I did not sleep before four o'clock in the morning. The next day I had already my travelling-cap on my head, when Augustine arrived; she was still paler than the previous night. Any one would have said she had not slept.

"'You are really going?' she said.

"'More than ever.'

"'By the diligence from the Lafitte office?'

"'Yes.'

"'At eleven o'clock precisely?'

"She began to smile as she asked the question.

"'What do you smile for?'

"'Nothing,' replied she; 'let us embrace, then, and a good journey to you.' I embraced her.

"'When shall you return?'

"'Who knows?'

"'In any case you will return here?'

"'Certainly.'

"'Adieu!'

"'Adieu, dear child!'

"At eleven o'clock I was in the *coupe* of the diligence, and there was only myself in it. My mother came to bid adieu to me, and the carriage had already started, when a commissionaire ran after the diligence, and, opening the door, said to me—

"'Monsieur Emmanuel de———?'

" 'That is my name,' said I.

" 'A letter for you, sir.'

" The man presented a note to me, and sprang back on to the pavement as the vehicle hurried on. I opened the note, which contained only these words :—

'My Dear Neighbour,—Bring me back a chaplet of beads from Rome; you, indeed, owe me that. I have sinned for you.

'Augustine.'

What sin had she committed? I was ignorant of it. I searched over in my mind; I could not discover it. I remembered well that exaggerated paleness in the morning, but that paleness could as much come from repentance as from sin.

" The result of my reflections," added Emmanuel, looking at me as he spoke, " was the decided opinion that I had been too delicate the previous evening. One hour after we changed horses at Charenton, and I had re-read that little perfumed note twenty times."

CHAPTER IV.

THE OLD LOVE AND THE NEW.

"You know what travelling is," continued Emmanuel "the novelty of what I saw about me made me almost forget Augustine; and it was but at Rome, in making my purchases, that I remembered the chaplet that she had asked me for, evidently more for the opportunity to avow her mental sin than for the purpose of asking me for a present. I therefore bought a very beautiful chaplet, which I put in my trunk with my other purchases; and I continued my tour. As I have already told you, when I arrived at Naples I made the acquaintance of Antonia and the remembrance of Augustine disappeared completely from my memory.

"I returned, you will remember, to Paris, with my danseuse; and after having sent my baggage to my rooms in the Rue Neuve des Mathurins, I installed myself almost completely with Antonia.

"I returned to sleep in the Rue Neuve des Mathurins but very rarely, and only when, on leaving the theatre, she told me she was fatigued, and that she was dull, as a danseuse often is after representations.

"Then there were the days when I passed the evening with my friends. On these days, or rather these nights, I returned to my own rooms, for I found it useless to go and wake up everybody in a house that was not my own, and to disturb Antonia—to carry to her the perfume of cigars and champagne.

"One night, it must have been one o'clock, I returned to the Rue Neuve des Mathurins. I was about to get into bed, when I fancied I heard some one rap. I thought that it was the wind shaking the door, and I did not open it; but the knock came a second time more distinctly. I declare to you I was far from suspecting the name of that nocturnal visitor. I thought that perhaps Antonia had sent her *femme de chambre* to seek for me. I rose up, and opened the door. It was Augustine in her night dress, as on the evening that preceded my departure.

"'Ah! it is you?' I said to her. And I took her hand.

"'You appear quite astonished to see me,' said she 'did you think that I was dead, or had entirely forgotten, you?' And she replied to the pressure of my hand with a lingering clasp. 'It is that hand,' said I, 'that wrote that delightful little note you sent after me to the diligence office?'

"'Yes,' she half murmured, whilst a timid blush stole over her face. Then I kissed her—I kissed her twice; and she looked at me with a tenderness that gave a new charm to every feature.

"'And my chaplet?' she inquired.

" 'Oh! I have it; here it is,' I cried, stooping down to my trunk, from which I took the chaplet.

" 'Why have you not sent it to me before now? Oh! it is magnificent, and I should only have liked better to have had the surprise sooner.' And sitting down, she examined and held up her present admiringly, with the delight of a child.

" 'At first I was afraid Monsieur Frederic would have inquired where you got it from, and would have importuned until you told him.'

" 'I am quite free to accept presents,' replied she, smiling, 'and I am not compelled to confess to him why I have asked for them, nor why they have been given to me.'

" A smile, the same that she must have had whilst writing the two lines that I quoted to you just now played continually on her lips; it was more than a smile, to me it was a revelation.

" 'I am but rarely here, and I had really forgotten this poor chaplet.'

" 'Ah!" she half whispered, with a sigh; 'love makes friendship orgotten.'

" 'What do you mean by that?'

" 'I mean, that since you have been in love, you no longer remember your friends.'

" 'Who has told you that I am in love?'

" 'Everybody.'

" 'Everybody occupies themselves about me!'

"'It is Frederic who has told me so.'

"'Where has he heard it, pray?'

"'At the club.'

"'Oh, indeed! and what did they say there?'

"'They say,' replied Augustine, with a trembling in her voice, 'that you have brought from Italy a marvel.'

"'That is true,' I answered, laughing; 'Antonia is very pretty.'

"'Ah! they call her Antonia?'

"'Yes.'

"'She's a professional dancer?'

"'Yes, she is.'

"'And it is a serious love?'

"'Very serious.'

"'Frankly, do you love her?'

"'Enormously.'

"Now, I must declare to you," said Emmanuel, interrupting his story, "I did not form any suspicion of Augustine's visit; none occurred to me. Therefore I paid no attention to—and did not study the replies I gave her. Silence followed my exaggerated confession of love, during which I searched my trunk, to see if I could find some other trinket to offer to my neighbour.

"'Stay,' said I, approaching her, "what do you think of this bracelet of antique medals?'

"It's very pretty,' she answered, listlessly, and almost without casting a look at it.

"'Will you accept it?' I inquired.

" 'You'd better keep it for Antonia.' There was some little bitterness in this remark; I could but turn and gaze at her face, as though seeking an interpretation of the tone given to her words.

" 'Come, take it,' I urged; 'you will afford me a great deal of pleasure.'

" 'Now, in point of fact,' said she, still speaking in the same tone, 'it is not beautiful enough to offer to a lady like her.'

" My dear child,' said I to Augustine, 'it has no other merit than that of having been bought at Rome, and of being made with antique medals. Now, I know that you like things with originality; that is the reason I beg you to accept it. As for Antonia she's a dancer and admires a glittering jewel better than a rare jewel without glitter.'

" 'Well, then,' said Augustine, 'I accept it.' Her hand, as she held it forth for the bracelet, glowed as on the evening of the day that I took my departure.

" 'You are feverish,' I remarked to hei; a slight assent with her hade was the only reply.

" 'It is late,' I conttnued; 'perhaps you ought to retire to rest?'

" 'Do I inconvenience you?'

" 'Are you mad?'

" 'Never mind; I must go—good night.' And she took her light from the mantelpiece. Spite of myself and my resolutions, I kept thinking of that night when she had quitted my chamber so suddenly. By a chance, perhaps a very natural one, Augustine's candlestick was in the same place as on that evening, and I, as on that evening, was sitting on my bed. I looked at her attentively; this conjunction of two identical incidents after a three months' absence threw retrospective thoughts and fancies into my mind. It seemed to me that Augustine did not leave the chamber with the same fixed resolution as on the former occasion. Looking at her, I saw that tears were brimming her eyelids, and I asked her 'What is the matter? You have some trouble.'

"'None at all.'

"'Has not Frederic returned?'

"'Yes, indeed, since it is he who has brought me the news of your return with Antonia.'

"'What is the matter, then?"

"'Nothing. Adieu.'

"I detained her by the arm, saying, 'Am I no longer your friend?' I spoke, influenced by a real friendship, and all eager to sympathise with the grief she might have, and desirous of consoling her to the best of my power. 'Come, then; come and sit by the side of me, and tell me all about it.' She a second time replaced her light upon the mantelpiece, and, led by me, without demur or hesitation, sat down with me where I had been sitting: She turned and looked in my face with quite a new look: and said, in a half-bantering tone—

"'Then she is very pretty?'

" 'There are moments when the mind is suddenly influenced by a trouble, when the tongue, scarcely knowing what it says, utters words it vainly fancies will disguise the real pain. Such were Augustine's words: 'Then she is very pretty t'

" 'Come, let us chat,' I sald to her; and thus speaking, passed my arm round her waist. I thought she would have forbidden me, but she contented herself by saying:

" 'If she saw you!'

" 'What could she do if she saw me?'

" 'You do really love her, then?'

" 'I love her, but what's that matter? What's that matter,' I repeated, 'if you but love me a little?'

" 'I!—I cannot have you as a lover. Now leave me; that wlll be better.'

" 'That will be better,' seemed to me strange; there was, then, the possibility of something else, since she said that it would be better that something else should not be. Nevertheless, the character of Augustine had, I thought so plainly evidenced itself at the commencement of our acquaintance that it appeared impossible for me to believe in so ready a construction of the past.

" 'No,' said she, to my caresses—'no; decidedly leave me. Let me go away,' she murmured—'you advised me to just now. I must, I will; pray let me!' At the same time, while seeming to strive to free herself from my arms, her head sank upon my shoulder. There was between our lips a distance of five thousand leagues, but surmountable in one second! I surmounted that distance; but she darted up from my arms as though stung, exclaiming:

"In the name of heaven, leave me alone!' This time it was too much. When a woman says, 'leave me alone,' you know, we consider he must be a blockhead who does so."

"'Ah!' said I to myself, 'Monsieur Frederic, you laughed at me the other night when I tumbled downstairs, I shall have a good laugh at you to-morrow when you come up."

"And since?" said I, interrupting Emmanuel.

"Since?" resumed Emmanuel, "at first I met Augustine frequently, but she always entreated me to forget that night, and cease not to implore me to keep my secret, adding, 'One day I shall release you from your silenee, for our adventure has been odd enough, and at some future time you may want to relate it."

"At length she came to tell me that she was leaving. I knew not till that moment how she had taken possession of my heart.

"'And you wish,' cried I, full of sadness, 'that it shall thus finish between us?"

"I do wish so,' she answered. 'But tell me again,' she added, with a smile that anticipated my reply; 'tell me again that you would have left Antonia for me.'

"I am ready to do so now!'

"Thanks,' she cried out; 'I love thee!' She kissed me; but ere I had woke from my surprise, she had disappeared. I never saw her again until the other evening at the ball at the opera; she had sent word to me to meet her there."

"Whatever for?"

"To release me from my promise of silence after Sunday. Frederic marries her on Saturday."

"Frederic marries her! What do you think of that?"

"I think," said Emmanuel, "that he's really a very lucky fellow."

ANTONIA, THE OPERA-DANCER.

ANTONIA,

THE OPERA DANCER.

I had my three histories; but, as you have seen, two only were known in all their detall; and the love-affair of Emmanuel and Antonia had been but merely indicated in the narration of these adventures. Scarcely had he said the last words that have been read, than he rose and ran out of the club, as if to escape from the many questions that I should have put to him. It appeared to me that the silence that he had almost effected to keep about Antonia, concealed some mysteries of his private life which must be curious to know; and since he had not told them to me, I promised myself to discover them, and to go and seek the monster even in his den. I knew the address of Emmanuel, who since he lived with a *danseuse* of renown, had thought himself obliged to give up his modest apartments in the Rue Neuve des Mathurius, and to replace it by a magnificent first floor in the Rue Taitbout. Some days after this second meeting, just narrated, I repaired to his house.

"Who do you want?" said the porteress.

"M. Emmanuel de——."

"He is not in."

"Is his domestic there?"

"No, sir."

"At what hour can Monsieur Emmanuel be found?"

"It is very rare that he is here."

"And his domestic?"

"He is almost never here."

I looked at the woman, and I thought that she was crazed.

"Pardon me, madame," I said to her, "but Monsieur Emmanuel de ——— is really a tenant of this house?"

"Yes, sir; his residence is here, but he does not stay here."

"Then, madame, will you tell me," replied I, with an exaggeration of politeness that ought to have given to the porteress a good opinion of my respect for the class of which she was a member; "will you tell me where is the house that Monsieur Emmanuel does not reside in, but where he stays?"

"I know nothing about it, sir; there is only his man-servant who can tell you about it." These replies sounded to me a little too much like bantering.

"But," exclaimed I, "since the domestic is almost always absent from here, how would you wish that I should find him?"

"If, sir, you will give me your name and your address, I will tell Alphonse to come and see you."

"The name of M. Emmanuel's servant, then, is Alphonse?"

"Yes, sir."

I gave the porteress my name and my address, and I added—

"Pray Monsieur Alphonse, if it will not inconvenience him too much, to come to me, and let me know where I can find M. Emmanuel, for I have something of importance to communicate to him."

"I will not fail to do so," said the woman. I returned home. Eight days slipped away without M. Alphonse appearing. I returned to the Rue Taitbout.

"Is M. Alphonse well?" inquired I of the porteress.

"Yes, sir, very well," was her reply, not recognising me immediateiy.

"Is he here?"

"No, sir."

"Ah! just so; he is never here, then?"

"He is very rarely here."

"And M. Emmanuel?"

"It is fifteen days since we have seen him," said the woman; then recognising me—"Oh! but you are the gentleman who cama eight days ago?"

"Yes; to whom you promised to send Alphonse."

"He has not been to you?"

"I have not seen him."

"He told me as much."

"That he should not come?"

"Yes."

"Why so?"

"He pretends he has not the time to inconvenience himself for all the friends of M. Emmanuel."

"He's rather an impertinent fellow, that Alphonse."

"Indeed he is."

"Therefore, there is no means of seeing M. Emmanuel nor M. Alphonse; nor of knowing where to find them, the one nor the other?"

"If you will promise me not to say that it was I who told you where he is, I will tell you where you can find M. Alphonse."

"You may rest satisfied of that."

"You promise me faithfully?"

"I give you my promise. You are very much afraid of him, then, I see."

"Oh! sir, everybody trembles before him in this house."

"I am the more curious to know him. Well, then, where is he?"

"He is at the wine-shop, on the left hand, at the end of the street."

"Thank you; I'll go there at once."

I went straight to the wine-shop. I found the master seated at his counter.

"Is M. Alphonse here?" I inquired of him.

"He is in the room at the back; he's at breakfast," replied the man.

"Would you tell him that there is someone here who would like to speak to him?"

" Alphonse !" cried the master of the wine-shop, openng the door of his back room, of which he had made a kind of private parlour.

" What !" replied a fretful voice, in the midst of the wine tipsy voices of several men.

" There is a gentleman who asks for you."

" Well, then, let him come in."

" Will you enter, sir?" the master said to me. This interview might as well be passed by; but this type of the domestic rather amused me. I entered.

" M. Alphonse, the domestic of M. Emmanuel de —?, said I, in entering.

This designation caused a great fellow to blush; who, raising his hand to his cap, more from habit than politeness, said to me—

" That's me, sir."

" Can you tell me where I shall find your master?"

" My master?" replied Alphonse, with fresh blushes; adding, with a leer, " he is with his little darling."

I blushed in my turn at the fashion in which this lacquey spoke of Emmanuel. Alphonse's comrades laughed at the intonation he had given to his facetiousness,

" Who do you call his little darling?" said I, with unmoved calmness; " is it a servant?" And I looked at M. Alphonse in a manner to let him understand that I would not suffer a second impertinence. I believe that these imbeciles submit, in spite of themselves, to the moral ascendancy; for this one, who was tall enough to eat four like myself, ceased his bantering tone, and, taking off his cap, said to me—

"M. Emmanuel de —— is with Mademoiselle Antonia, Rue de Provence, No. 19."

I raised my hand to my hat, and went out. I proceeded at once to No. 19, Rue de Provence. I ascended to the floor the porter indicated—the third floor—and rang at a door covered with green velvet, set round with gilt nails, and ornamented with a handle of crystal.

"M. Emmanuel de ——," said I to the femme de chambre, who came and opened it to me—"is he here?"

"No, sir," replied the girl, with a certain hesitation.

"Mademoiselle Antonia, is she here?"

"Neither is she."

"Have the kindness to hand this card to M. Emmanuel when he returns."

"Yes, sir."

The femme de chambre shut the door. I descended slowly, for I was convinced that the announcement of M. Emmanuel's absence was but an order, and that he would come and call me back as soon as they had given him my card. I had not gone down twenty steps when I heard his voice.

"Come back," he cried to me from the top of the stairs, "come back! I am always at home for you."

I turned back, and remounted the stairs.

"It is very kind of you to come to see me," he said, giving me his hand.

"I have had trouble enough to find this address," I could not refrain from saying.

"You had but to ask it at my rooms."

"That's what I have done."

Whilst speaking, Emmanuel led me into an elegant boudoir, hung with yellow brocade, and had made me sit down by the fire.

"Well, then," rejoined he, "they told you directly where you could find me."

"There is only your domestic that knows."

"Alphonse?"

"Just so. He is a very insolent fellow, that M. Alphonse," said I.

Emmanuel passed his hand over his forehead with an impatient gesture, and continued—

"Well, after all, he gave you the address of Antonia?'

"Yes."

"That's all right."

As it appeared to be disagreeable to Emmanuel to speak of his domestic, I did not open my mouth any more about him.

"Do you know, you are indeed splendid here!" said I to him, to change the conversation.

"Yes, just now; I will show you the rest when Antonia has gone to the rehearsal."

Just then the femme de chambre opened the door.

" Sir," said she to Emmanuel, " Madame inquires for you."

" Wait for me an instant," said Emmanuel to me, and he rose and went out.

I waited, looking at the thousand useless things which compose the boudoir of women in general, and *danseuses* in particular. At the expiration of about ten minutes I heard the doors of the passage from the dining-room and the saloon close noisily, and Emmanuel reappeared, with an irritated, or rather, I should say, an unhappy air.

" I inconvenience you, perhaps," said I ; " I will go."

" On the contrary, remain, and as long as you can."

He sat down with a sigh, and taking up the tongs, began to stir the fire, like a man pre-occupied, and who does not know wnat he is doing.

" Antonia has gone out ?" I inquired of him, breaking the silence.

" She has just gone."

" Is she rehearsing a new ballet?"

" I believe so."

" That does not appear to interest you much."

" In reality, I am quite indifferent about it." There was a ring at the door.

" Be quiet," said Emmanuel to me in a low voice.

" You do not receive any one, then ?"

" No," said Emmanuel, listening.

Five minutes after the femme de chambre appeared.

" It is Madame's dressmaker," she said to Emmanuel.

"Well, you have told her that Madame has gone out?"

"Yes, sir; she says she will return this evening."

Emmanuel uttered a new sigh, and the servant left the room.

"Well, let us see the apartments," I then said.

"Come," said Emmanuel. He rose, and I followed him. We entered the saloon; it was decorated in white, cherry-colour, and gold.

"It is you who have given this saloon to Antonia?" I asked.

"Yes; it is I who have given her all that there is here. Do you think this saloon handsome?"

"Superb!"

"Here is her chamber," said Emmanuel, opening a door.

And we entered a chamber hung with blue damask, the furniture of which was in rosewood, and the curtains made of Venice guipure, the dearest of all guipures.

"The devil!" exclaimed I; "it is impossible to be better than this."

"Is not this chamber pretty?" said Emmanuel, as if my reply in the affirmative ought to console him some little for his dejected mood.

"It is enchanting!"

"You have seen the *salle a manger*?"

"In tapestry and carved oak?"

"Yes."

"It is very beautiful."

"That's all, my dear fellow."

"And plenty, too. And it has cost—— ?"

"In all?"

"Yes, in all."

"Fifty-seven thousand francs."

"And it's paid for?"

"Alas! no."

There was a ring again at the door. We heard the servant talking for some moments with the visitor; then the door was shut.

"It is the job-master, from whom the carriages are hired," said the girl, opening the door of the saloon.

"You have told him that I was not in?"

"Yes, sir."

"What did he say?"

"That he would come again to-morrow."

We returned into the boudoir. I sat down. I felt that I should like to know the cause of that profound sadness in which Emmanuel seemed plunged. I perhaps pretty well guessed it, but I was wishing to learn it from himself. I resumed:

"You never go to the Rue Taitbout?"

"Never."

"Why not?"

"What should I go there for?"

"You are wrong to keep a domestic. That Alphonse drinks your wine at the wine shop—"

"I know that very well."

"Why do you not discharge him?"

"Can I do so?"

"Why not?" And after a moment's hesitation, I said "You owe him money?"

"Yes."

"A great deal?"

"A great deal."

"How much?"

"Four thousand francs."

"How is it," I said, with undisguised surprise, "that you owe four thousand francs to your domestic?'

"He has lent me three thousand."

"What! you have borrowed money from that man?"

"I have been obliged to; and you understand now why I dare not say anything to him. Without him I should have gone to a debtor's prison."

"I saw at a glance how it was. I bowed down my head.

"Antonia knew all this?" continued I.

"Yes."

"What did she say to you?"

"She got up some scenes."

"To——?"

"To have money, by Jove!"

"And you have none?"

"There is not twenty francs here."

"And your mother?"

"My mother! I am at variance with her."

"You must break away from this life, my dear fellow," said I.

"Find the means," was his answer. "My mother will not give me a sou; I can no longer find anyone to lend me money; and I am thirty thousand francs in debt."

There was another ring at the door. This time the visitor would not be dismissed like the two preceding ones, and, after some altercation, I heard him exclaim—

"I know that your master is here; and I will not go without speaking with him."

"That one," half-whispered Emmanuel, with another sigh, "that one is the jeweller."

It made me pity him. A third time the girl opened the door.

"It is the jeweller," said she, in an undertone.

"I know it."

"He will not go."

"Good. Leave us."

Emmanuel thrust his hands into his pockets, and walked to and fro, like a man who is becoming insane. As I looked at him, I began to understand suicide for debt. Moved by his embarrassed position, I said to him—

"Will you let me go and speak to the man?"

He leaped at my proposition, exclaiming, "Do! Just so—go!" not concealing his joy at this help.

"What shall I say to him?"

"Anything you like, provided that he'll go, and that I do not see him. Here it is fifty times that I have made him call."

I left the boudoir. I found the jeweller seated in the *salle a manger*. I went up to him; I was rather embarrassed. He rose up.

"Sir," said I, "M. Emmanuel cannot receive you at this moment."

"But, sir," said the honest tradesman—who had evidently charged Emmanuel fifty per cent too dear, and who was as importunate as if he had sold at the manufacturer's price—"this affair must be closed. M. de —— has owed me six thousand francs for a year past, and I have never yet received a sou. I will not go until he gives me something on account, were it but one hundred francs."

I knew that Fmmanuel had but twenty francs in the house, and I did not want to tell him that I had not the hundred francs myself.

"M. Emmanuel is unwell," I urged. "He has not that sum heie," said I to the jeweller, almost in a supplicating tone; "if he had, he would give it you directly, I know. His affairs are about to be arranged; let me beg of you to have a little patience—there shall be no delay. I engage that he will send you something on account within the next eight days."

The creditor wavered, and I struck the last blow.

"There must be a little indulgence for young men," I resumed; "they buy without bargaining, and without well knowing what they really do: It is for others, you trade gentlemen, to be more reasonable than they are. I shall speak this evening of your debt to Emmanuel's mother, and, I assure you, you shall soon have a satisfactory reply."

"That which irritates me," said the jeweller, "is not so much that he is in my debt, but that he will never receive me. If I saw M. de——, I should take patience; but I am humiliated to meet servants only, who reply to me, 'Sir, he is not within;' or, 'He has just gone out;' or, 'He is in the country;' when I know positively tha he is in his chamber."

"You are right," said I, "that is bad; I shall expostulate with M. Emmanuel about it."

"Well, then, I count on your good offices, sir?"

"Make yourself easy."

"Within eight days?"

"Within eight days."

And, with a profound bow, the jeweller took his departure.

"Well," said Emmanuel, as I re-entered.

"He's gòne," said I.

"How much I thank you," said he, taking my hand.

"Oh!" said I, jocularly, "I know all about that."

"What have you said to him?"

"I have spoken to him. To speak to a creditor is to

give him something on account, you know ; yet, do really try to send him something."

"Do you think that if I could I would not pay them all, even if I lived on bread and water for a year?"

"But you have some rents?"

"Two houses."

"Raise some money on them."

"Is it not already done? And my mother has led me to know, for I never see her, that she will interdict me if I contract a new loan."

"How can you live with these torments?"

"Ah! I don't know."

"You must love Antonia, then, very much?"

"I have never loved her, that is what makes it the more frightful; you know very well why I brought her to Paris, that it was but to make Henriette enraged; vengeance for which I am well punished to-day. I have spent money with Antonia to have the air of being in love; and, from being so, I have arrived at where I am."

"You did not tell me that at the opera."

"And I should never have told you, if you had not seen it yourself. I blush at the life that I lead."

"You must get away from it."

"How? I have already said that it is impossible."

"Let us reason the question nevertheless."

"That will do no good."

"You are at the end of your resources?"

"I am."

"You tell me you have not twenty francs."

"That's true."

"Let us look at it in the worst light. To-morrow you will not have a sou?"

"That is true again."

"What shall you do? You will die of hunger."

"No; because I shall find somebody to lend me one hundred francs, two hundred francs, or fifty francs, among my friends—my tailor, my bootmaker—who knows me, and the house will keep on. I shail take a box; I shall take Antonia to the theatre; and I shall have peace for four or five days. That's a good deal, four or five days of tranquillity. That is how I have lived these three months past; and the proof that one becomes accustomed to all, even to this dishonourable life, is that which I have gone through to-day; for if they had told me two years back I should come to have thus lived, I believe that I should have preferred to have burnt my brains at once. Nobody knows what a woman without heart can do with a man without energy. Terrible it is to say; but one more year of this problematical existence, and I believe I should arrive at acceding to any means, without exception, whereby to procure money."

"If Antonia loved you, even a little, she would reduce her expenses."

"If she loved me as Juliet loved Romeo, she could not do that which you say."

"Why not?"

"What do you call reducing the expenses?"

"How many domestics have you?"

"Four. A *femme de chambre*, who dresses Antonia at the theatre; a cook, a groom, and a valet, without counting Alphonse."

"You could do away with two."

"Which?"

"The groom and the valet."

"I owe five hundred francs to the one, and fifteen hundred francs to the other; with what can I pay them?"

"You have a carriage?"

"Hired at six hundred francs a month."

"Dismiss it."

"Eighteen hundred francs is owing where it is hired. The man was here for payment just now, and if the carriage is not kept on he will not leave the house until the debt is paid."

"What is the rent here?"

"Three thousand francs."

"Remove; and Antonia must content herself with an apartment at a thousand francs."

"There's six months' rent owing, and it's on a lease of three years."

"Your apartment in the Rue Taitbout is not used?"

"Only to lodge M. Alphonse."

"Have you a lease there?"

"No."

"Quit that lodging, then, and sell the furniture."

"The furniture is already seized by my creditors."

"Leave them to sell it."

"That shall be done, but delay as much as possible the inevitable moment by paying expenses and giving bills; but this method of delay cannot be continued, for the bills must be dishonoured."

"Have you the firm intention to break off from Antonia?"

"Yes."

"To leave also, if it is necessary?"

"Yes."

"Well, then, go and find your mother, and tell her to yet make another sacrifice of ten thousand francs. You do not want more than that to temporarily escape from your embarrassment."

"She will refuse me."

"No."

"Here it is already three times that I have employed that means to get money."

"Then it must be abandoned now."

"But there are no other means."

"You have no inclination to throw yourself into the water?"

"I shall not reply to you."

"Do you wish that I should make Antonia hear reason?"

"I defy you to do that."

"Do you wish at least that I should try?"

"What shall you say to her?"

"What does that matter, provided that you are extricated? Shall I come and see her to-morrow morning?"

"Come, rather, this evening. I shall go out, and she will be alone."

"Can you not go out to-morrow morning?"

"No."

"Why not? You can't amuse yourself much here."

"That's true; but I cannot go out before sunset."

"You are pursued?"

"I have the pleasure, when I open the curtains of my window, of seeing the sheriff's officers waiting for me."

"They never enter here?"

"They do; but I am saved by the servants' staircase; and as the lease is in Antonia's name, and she has declared to them that she does not know me, they dare not come up again."

"How you must regret the time with Henriette!"

"With a bitterness that has no words to express it; there are days, or rather I should say evenings, when I go and walk below her windows, to revive my hope a little with the remembrance of the past. Ah! I forgot to tell you, Antonia has a mother—and such a mother my dear fellow!"

CHAPTER II.

A SWORN PROMISE.

"THERE are things which the world knows not, that it cannot know; such as that to those who unfortunately enter, either by taste or through unrestrained freedom—which latter cause is the more frequent—into a life like that Emmanuel led, a moment at length arrives when the apparently trifling obstacles of which I am about to speak close one upon the other in such rapid succession, in such strength, and forming a circle so binding, that no vantage ground is left from which spring can be taken to leap and clear the barrier which defies escape. We are no longer in the patriarchal times when Abraham sent Hagar away, giving her a pitcher of water and a measure of wheat. To-day, when a young man has lived with a French actress; when he is ruined by her; when he has taken a lodging on a fifth story, whilst he has furnished for her a splendid apartment; when he has brutalised his youth and stained his name with her; when he has used up his last resources to satisfy her caprices; when he has placed his liberty, his happiness, his fortune, under the dependency of a creature full of vanity and corruption; when he has estranged himself from his family and from all the affections of his childhood; when he covers her with jewels like a Spanish Madonna, and has covered himself with debt;--you fancy, perhaps, that when the day arrives that unequivocally proves to him that he has no more to give her, that he is free to leave her; and, more, that he may at least have confidence to say to her, 'We are quits!' Error! She will be the most eager amongst his creditors, the most terrible of his enemies; herself not loving him, she will make a weapon of his love; she will pursue him with scandals and menaces, attacking even his honour, placing his life in jeopardy. His intimacy with her will lead him into lawsuits and duels; and he never can completely wipe away the mire into which he has fallen. She will not scruple to let it be known that the unfortunate has lived up to his income; she will seek to dishonour him by his very bounty to herself; and all this under the very mask of the beautiful sentiments of one injured; and thus, as a bravo, she will strike him in every corner where he is driven. She will assert that she has sacrificed for him chances, successes, position in the world—because, she will say, "I loved him;" and she finds men who believe her, who pity her, and who, when they pass him in the street, point the finger of scorn. All the past time that he has known her has been one of shameful servitude; he has had to render to her a faithful account of the least actions of his life; whilst he has seen all his good sentiments, all his young and enthusiastic soarings pass away one after the other; for he had not even the excuse of love. He has taken that woman for pleasure, and he retains her for self-pride. And the day after he leaves her, he learns that she has deceived him; that the very domestics, who owe to him their bread, were her accomplices; that letters have passed under his eyes, and assignations carried on where he had no suspicion. He discovers that the rehearsal tickets and headaches were but fictions to excuse absence or send him away. But the day that he learns all this, he is so elated with having broken away—the very air of freedom seems so inspiriting—that he no longer cares about her; he finds himself so happy that, whatever the cost, it is cheap to be rid of her.

"Before this day has arrivrd there is yet a period when the heart asks how it could have passed a part of life thus, full of self-scorn; that these, the best years and the purest, should have been given up to withering corruption. What is yet more terrible to relate is, that anything that woman does is not premeditated; she has no intention of ruining you; she has not the intention of compromising you. Her actions are the consequence of the wants, the fears, the weariness of the life she leads; she obeys the counsel of the creatures who compose her acquaintance, and from whom you strive in vain to isolate her; for there is always a moment when, like a madman, you believe seriously, or fancy that she loves you, and that the love which you inspire tends to purify her. Now she knows but one thing, which is, that she has a lover who has the stupidity of assuming the responsibility of her life; and, to keep him, she employs every means within her reach. If she desires to make her lover marry her, she will boldly seek to carry out her views! and, should he have no other means of gaining peace, he will finish by adopting this one. In the meantime she tells, on all sides, that the marriage is an affair concluded; and she gains for him the reputation of an idiot, who defames to a girl of that sort the honourable name that he has received from his father."

"There is just where I am," said Emmanuel, interrupting me at this point of my discourse, for I had repeated the foregoing remarks to him. "Antonia goes everywhere, saying on all sides that I am about to marry her. I leave her to say so to avoid disturbances. There are days when, like to-day, I have not twenty francs, and when I do not know how ever I shall procure money; a silk-merchant or a lace-merchant comes, and Antonia buys or orders fifteen or eighteen hundred francs worth with the same cool indifference as though she had but to open her drawer to pay for every extravagance. And if I leave unpaid this debt, and many others contracted in the same fashion, I shall pass for a dishonest man in the eyes of those tradesmen, who only sell to her because they know that I am here, and make myself answerable for what she buys."

Emmanuel became silent, and let his head fall into his hands.

I was about to reply to him.

"Oh! I know well enough what you are about to say to me again," rejoined he, without moving; "you are going to tell me that it will be well that all this should finish at once, and you are about to recommence giving me counsels. Give me as much as you will, I only advise you beforehand that they will be useless."

"You are mistaken," said I; "it is not such that I wish to say to you."

"Speak, then."

"Promise me, that if you had the money to pay all that you owe, and to leave Antonia honourably, you would leave her?"

"I would."

"You swear it?"

"I swear it."

"Then I will have that money."

"How?"

"What does that matter, provided that I have it?"

"But do you know how much I must have?"

"You must have thirty thousand francs."

"At the least."

"You shall have it."

"To whom are you going to ask for it?"

"Do you wish to know?"

"I do."

"To your mother."

"She will refuse you."

"I am sure of the contrary."

"When shall you see her?"

"To-day. It is better than seeing Antonia, and endeavouring to make her hear reason. Call your creditors together, and give them fifteen thousand francs; you will ask time from them, a year for instance, for the payment of the rest; you will leave Antonia without a debt; you will put five thousand francs for her in her drawer, to give her time to wait your successor, which will not be long; you will pay M. Alphonse, and you will kick him out at the door; you will pay the claim on your furniture, which you will then sell; and with that which remains, you will go and live for three or four months in Italy, or in Africa, that New Belgium for ruined French gentlemen, that you may not have here the vexation which always results from a separation, and which you know so well. Does that suit you?"

"Perfectly."

"You approve of my step?"

"I fear but one thing, that it will not succeed."

"I shall see that to-morrow."

"Why not this evening?"

"Because it is not certain that I should find your mother at home. Besides, Antonia would be here, and we cannot talk at our ease."

"To-morrow, then; but silence."

"Keep yourself easy; to-morrow, then, at two o'clock, I shall be here; you will wait for me?"

"With impatience."

"Your mother lives always in the same place?"

"Always."

"Rue de Verneuil?"

"Yes; No. 26."

I took leave of Emmanuel, and repaired at once to the Rue de Eerneuil. Madame de —— was not at home. I returned the day following at one o'clock. I was announced; as I entered Madame de —— was sitting by the fireside, reading. She was a woman of about forty five years of age; as she looked up from her book, I saw at a glance that her face was full of benevolence, and the distinguishing air of a gentlewoman. Her hair, already grey, was arranged in broad folds; she wore a cap with pink velvet ribbons, and was dressed in myrtle green. I had not the honour of being known to her, and at once hastened to say to her, as an excuse for my visit—

"Madame, I am a friend of Emmanuel's."

"Something, then, has happened to him?" she immediately said, with an anxiety of expression that seemed to augur well for my mission. She closed her book, and placed it on the mantelpiece.

"No, madame, happily, such is not the case," I quickly replied.

The face of Emmanuel's mother darkened a little.

"Then to what do I owe your visit, sir?" continued she, in a tone that a little discouraged me.

I came plainly to the question.

"Madame," said I, "Emmanuel is very unhappy."

"Through his own fault, sir.'

"That is true; but, for some cause that exists, he is so."

"Well, sir, what would you that I should do?"

"I would, madame, or, rather, I desire—I wish, that you will for the last time rescue him from his embarrassment."

"That is impossible, sir: Emmanuel has fifteen thousand pounds in rents of his own; he has borrowed in such fashion, and at so high a rate, that the interest he pays absorbs his income, and the sum borrowed already touches his capital. Three times he has had recourse to me; three times have I assisted him, counting always that he would hold to the word that he gave me, that he would change his manner of life, for the life that he leads is degrading; three times he has broken his word. These sort of things are, perhaps, very droll in comedies. To deceive a mother for the benefit of an opera girl; to force her to economise where she has not been in the habit of doing so, to content the caprices of a dancing girl;-all that is, perhaps, a received and accepted thing in the world where Emmanuel now lives, but it is a custom of which I will neither be the dupe nor the victim. I have thirty thousand francs in rents; he is my only child; he can wait for my death, or he can borrow upon it, as he sees best. For myself, I am resolved not to make any change in my mode of life for my son, since he has resolved not to change anything in his for me. We shall see if he steps aside from such mode of life, if he proves his repentance to me in any way;—but until such moment I shall remain inflexible."

Emmanuel's mother was silent. Then I commenced to detail to her all those little and terrible obstacles which he had contracted, and which bound him, as the cords of the Lilliputians bound the giant Gulliver upon his back. I explained to her, not without a certain difficulty, how the life of idleness and dissoluteness had only with Emmanuel reached one step, and endeavoured to show her that the misfortune was not beyond reparation, and hat the moment for this would arrive; assuring her that it was only from certain considerations of self-delicacy that he did not at once abandon Antonia, for whom he entertained feelings of hatred, and even of contempt. I gave her as pathetic a picture as possible of the perpetual fears in the midst of which my friend was forced to live, and which would finish by ruining him—not only in his fortune, but in his intellect and health.

"You must admit, sir," said Madame de ——, interrupting me, and wiping away her tears, "that it is indeed painful for the heart of a mother to be separated from her son for such reasons. Emmanuel's father is dead, and his mother is alone, without family, and she had but one pleasure, but one recreation—that was her son. He left that mother to go and live with an opera-dancer. And now, his mother, if she wishes to go out anywhere, she must seek the arm of a stranger ; if she enters a theatre, she sees Mademoiselle Antonia in a box with her son, who hides himself—be it that he fears his mother shall see him, or be it that he fears he shall be obliged to come and greet her.

"All the gentlemen whom I know," she continued, "and who know of this as well as I do, and who are pained by this scandalous existence, proffer me their condolence, and pity me ; so much so, that to spare these poignant conversations, I am reduced to see only those who are considerate enough not to speak more of Emmanuel than if he were dead ; that is to say, I live almost alone. You speak of Emmanuel's griefs ! What would you say to mine, sir, did you know them ?"

The poor lady wept whilst saying this, and I understood immediately how culpable Emmanuel was in her sight. She went on—

"Why must my son have any delicacy in quitting a woman who is his ruin ?—he who has not understood that the first delicacy to which a man ought to bend, is that which consists in not making a future of sorrow to a mother who has made him a past of joy and of pleasure Know I not as well as you, sir, what terrible consequences Emmanuel's follies involve ? If do not know them in their details, my heart divines them in their results. Every day I tremble to hear it announced that Emmanuel has been engaged in a duel, and that he is wounded, perhaps dead—or some news yet more terrible.

When I saw you enter just now, and you told me that you were a friend of my son's, I thought I should have fallen ill. When I think that the least of the sorrows that I have to dread is that my son may be completely ruined! You are going to see Emmanuel again, sir; you will tell him what you have seen; that I do not speak his name without tears, and that it is not impossible that I can be more wretched than I am!"

To repeat, after this, the request I had made on entering was a rather difficult affair. Meanwhile I was convinced that the happiness of Emmanuel and of his mother depended on this last sacrifice. I recalled to myself that which I should see when returning to my friend. This recollection gave strength to my resolution, and I added—

"Well, madame, I can only hope that one day you may have to thank me for the visit that I have the honour to pay you now; and I should desire above all that it was not unavailing to the peace of Emmanuel. He requires but a very small sum—"

"What, sir," Madame de —— interrupted me afresh, "do you think that the refusal is with me a question of money? I would give the half, the three-quarters of my fortune, my fortune itself, for Emmanuel's happiness. I would give my life for him; but on condition that the happiness that resulted should be a real happiness—legal, legitimate; on the condition that this happiness should not consist in giving diamonds and cashmeres to an opera-girl. And surely it is also impossible," she exclaimed, "with the education he has received, that Emmanuel can place his happiness open to these daily scandals! How much will rescue Emmanuel from this entanglement?—thirty, forty, fifty thousand francs? Oh heavens! If he will come and live with me, if he will remember that he has a mother, if he will live within his income, have honourable friends—in two hours he shall have those fifty thousand francs; but that I will aid in trailing my name in the mire, and by my feebleness encourage him in his ruin, that will finish but with my own, that shall not be—that is what I will never do!"

There was a hope to be conceived in the last part of this interruption of Madame de ——. I seized it.

"Well, then, Madame," said I, at once, "I can say that to Emmanuel?'

"You can, sir."

"That he quits Antonia, and that he comes and lives here, and—"

"Ah! you go too fast, sir. I know Emmanuel; he will come and live here, and he will leave in eight days after the old debts are paid, and he can go and make new ones. He requires a lesson that must be received. We have a little country seat in Touraine; he can come there to pass three or four months with me, and I will pay all his debts. Does that appear to you too exacting?"

"Certainly not, madame."

"As well as which," added Madame de ——, "we shall have delightful country neighbours, and Emmanuel can amuse himself well. That is what I will do, and you will understand it at once; it is to remove him for some itme from the acquaintance, both of men and of women, that he has contracted in Paris. When he has had a tranquil existence with respectable people for three or four months, he will feel a contempt for those who have so long estranged him from myself; and there will, I believe, be a transformation in him. Are you, sir, of my opinion?"

"Perfectly, madame, I am."

"Well, then, sir, carry to him my propositions of peace."

"I am engaged to see him immediately, madame; and I can assure you that to-morrow evening he shall be seated by your hearth."

"That is my wish, sir," said Madame de ——, wiping the tears from her eyes, in which shone the sweet sunshine of maternal hope.

I took leave of Emmanuel's mother, whom I left a little calmer than she had been during the course of our conversation; and I hastened at once to our hero, to announce to him the happy result of my visit. Whilst raising my hand to the bell at Antonia's door I heard loud bursts of laughter in the house. I recognised distinctly the voices of the domestics.

"What a well-kept house!" said I, giving a sigh; and

I rang the bell. The servant came and opened the door.

"M. Emmanuel is here?" inquired I, entering, not making any doubt but that he was.

"No, sir," replied the girl.

"No! Then he will return soon?"

"No, sir, he is at Havre with Madame."

"At Havre!—for how long?"

"For eight days, sir."

"Now, really," cried I to myself, staggered by this announcement, "this is too bad!"

CHAPTER III.

GOOD NEWS.

So thunderstruck was I by Emmanuel's departure, that I knew not what step to take. "And he has left no word or message for me?" I inquired.

"No, sir, none."

"Do you know at what hotel he stays at Havre?"

"I don't know ar all," replied the girl; "but if you will speak to Madame d'Orimont, she is here."

"Who is Madame d'Orimont?" said I.

"It is the mother of Mademoiselle."

"Well, then, tell her I should be glad to say two words to her."

The servant showed me into the boudoir; and some moments after Antonia's mother appeared. She had neither the Tartan shawl, nor the cap, nor the workbag, which are held as the characteristic features of the French actress's mother. She did not appear to be more than forty years of age, and was very elegantly dressed. She must once have been very pretty. She had blonde hair, arranged in the English style. It was easy to be seen that she bestowed great care on her toilet. She wore a robe of pearl grey silk, and a little quilled bonnet, fit for a girl of fifteen. She had brilliant diamond earrings, and diamond rings sparkled on her white hands, that she rubbed continually together to make still whiter. She had thrown an Indian cashmere over her shoulders; and the first thing she did on entering the room was to approach the glass, readjust the fold of her dress, and of her collar; after which she turned round and asked me with a smile, and in a tone half of ceremony, half of familiarity, what I desired. At the same time she sat down, bidding me be seated.

Madame d'Orimont had thrown herself upon a small sofa, with the air of a woman habituated to satin-covered furniture, and said to me, stretching out her feet—which, by the way, were small, and in elegant blue boots, with varnished leather toes—

"You wished to speak to me, sir?"

"Yes, madame," I rejoined, "I seek news of Emmanuel, who appointed to meet me this morning, and whom I expected to find here."

"He is at Havre with my daughter," replied Madame d'Orimont, playing with the ringlets of her hair, and speaking through her lips, doubtless to hide her teeth, which she would have shown to me, like her feet, had they been beautiful ones.

"I know it, madame, and it is that which astonishes me."

"And why does that astonish you, sir?"

"It astonished me at first, madame, because I had to

return a reply to Emmanuel on a rather important affair; afterwards, because I knew him to be very embarrassed, and I did not believe that he had the necessary money to take a journey—even so short a journey as this."

"Antonia has eight days of liberty; she has longed to see Havre, which she does not know; I have lent five hundred francs to Emmanuel."

"And he has accepted them?" sald I, with wonderment.

"Why not? Oh! it is not the first time that I have lent money to him; he owes me also two or three thou sand francs; but what has that to do with it?'

I was, I might say, perfectly stunned and bewildered.

"However," continued Madame d'Orimont, "he is an amiable young man. Have you known him a long time?"

"I was at college with him," I responded, mechanically.

"He is very gentle, and I am quite content that my daughter lives with him. She could have made a richer acquaintance, it is true, but she would not have loved him, whilst she loves Emmanuel."

"Then Emmanuel will not return for eight days?"

"Oh, good heavens! no. During their absence I come to see a little what passes here, and to overlook and take care of the house, for those two poor children have no order; but I suppose I shall finish by comingto live with them."

"If Emmanuel's mother," thought I to myself, "only knew that her son had borrowed money from that woman, what grief would be hers!"

"What are you thinking of now?" said Madame d'Orimont, breaking my momentary reverie.

"I am thinking of what you have told me, madame, and of the interest you appear to take in Emmanuel."

"Oh? I love him very much, I assure you. He's a fellow of intelligence and spirit, and I am sure that on his side he has a real affection for me. He has confidence in me as in his own mother."

"What desecration of noble words!" I said to myself.

"Well, then, madame," rejoined I, rais ng my voice, and with the endeavour to obtain the solution of the character of this woman, "since you love Emmanuel and your daughter so much, there is a counsel you ought to give them."

"What is that?"

"It is that they should s parate."

"Are you mad!" cried Madame d'Orimont. "Antonia would die; she loves Emmanuel to foolishness, and he adores her; why should they separate?"

"Emmanuel has not the necessary fortune to live with Mademoiselle Antonia."

"But, sir, my daughter spends nothing belonging to your friend," replied Madame d'Orimont, in rather a sharp tone. "Never has my daughter spent so little money; and the little that she has spent I have given to her, for your friend, Emmanuel, is entirely without any means."

"Then, madame, you ought to be the first to understand that this state of things cannot last. Your daughter suffers from it, and her future becomes lost to her. Since she is young and beautiful, she will easily find a better position than that which Emmanuel can offer her."

"That is true, sir; but Emmanuel will not leave her. If you only knew what scenes we have had together! He wished to marry her, but it was I who would not allow it."

"And you did well, madame, in preventing it."

"Without doubt I did," assented Madame d'Orimont, who mistook the sense of my words; "you can understand my not letting my daughter marry the young man; he has not fortune sufficient for her; she can find a better."

It is scarcely to be credited, yet it is true, that the mothers of such as Antonia have always the conviction that their child will one day marry a prince or an honest man. Unhappily, there are three or four precedents by which their hopes are sustained. I looked at Madame d'Orimont when she had ceased speaking, and my impression was that she had spoken in sincerity.

"Yes," she resumed, "I have had trouble enough to prevent this marriage."

I could see that it was best for me to seem as if joining in Madame d'Orimont's singular view of the affair, thinking perhaps that in thus turning to account her interested reasons, she might prove a powerful aid to the wishes of Emmanuel's mother in effecting a rupture.

"So it is you, madame," I exclaimed, "who have the goodness to keep house when Emmanuel has been without money?"

"Yes, sir."

"You have, then, a large fortune?"

"No. I have a hundred thousand francs, all that my husband, the Count d'Orimont, left me after his death. I brought him a fine marriage portion, that he nearly ate up. Antonia had a taste for dancing; I caused her to enter at the opera, and now she has an independent position. We ought to have had twenty-five thousand pounds in rents, if her father had not led so dissipated a life."

Nothing on the part of Madame d'Orimont any longer astonished me. For a long time I have known this type of mother; and I was quite prepared to hear her say that she was descended from Robert Bruce; for in France it is always from the great Scottish chief that those who are descended from nobody trace their descent.

"Mademoiselle Antonia," inquired I, in the endeavour to arrange the questions and the replies in such a manner as to draw from Madame d'Orimont that which I was desirous that she should avow to me, "Mademoiselle Antonia became acquainted with Emmanuel at Naples."

"Where she lived with the Duke de Pololi, who wished to marry her."

"He also!"

"He also. There was also a great piece of scandal there. The Duke had not attained his majority, and his family obtained from the King of Naples an order to make us quit the town; but I knew the French consul and the English consul—and we did not leave until we chose to do so. Antonia held on to the family; she had a child by the Duke; and, when I threatened to make a noise, the Prince Pololi consented to give a pension to the child."

"And what has become of the infant?"

"Unfortunately, it is dead."

"And the pension?"

"Has been suppressed."

"Then the Duke de Pololi was Mademoiselle Antonia's first lover?"

"Nearly so. She had only had as a lover the old Lord Bullston, whom you know, perhaps?"

"No, I do not know him."

"Oh! he is very rich; he's a charming man. He's enormously fat. He was her first lover. He was such a well-behaved man. It was he that gave me all that I have."

Madame d'Orimont bit her lips, but it was too late; I pretended not to have heard her last revelation.

"You know," she immediately continued, "my

daughter has sacrificed all for Emmanuel, and he cannot leave her without securing her an income."

"There we are!" said I to myself.

"It is only two months ago," pursued Madame d'Orimont (it was in the month of October), the Prince Korloff offered to Antonia an engagement for Russia, and an income of ten thousand roubles. She refused.

"On account of Emmanuel?"

"On account of Emmanuel. I could show you his letters—charming letters. The prince loved me and esteemed me much. Every day I regret him."

"He is dead?"

"No, he has returned to Russia. The emperor recalled him."

I saw in what a mesh the poor fellow was taken. They had finished by persuading him that he had ruined not only the daughter, but the mother also; and this in ruining himself. See, then, to what ends they can make a man's delicacy serve.

"But yet, madame, if to-morrow Emmanuel had no more money, and no hopes of any more, it would be better that he separated from your daughter."

"There is no fear of that," replied Madame d'Orimont; "he has money; he has told us so. His mother has thirty thousand pounds in rents, which cannot be removed from her son."

"But his mother is not disposed to die."

"But he can borrow upon his inheritance."

"That is difficult to do."

"No; and I believe also, that a few days hence I shall have found a loan of forty thousand francs for Emmanuel. I know a gentleman who will lend him them if I give my signature."

"It is absolutely necessary," thought I, "that I see Emmanuel at once; with the bait of this money they will make him do whatever they wish; and heaven knows what they will make him do!"

"You understand," said Madame d'Orimont, "he will receive forty thousand francs, less the premium, the debt being reimbursed; but at the death of Emmanuel's mother, of course the lender must gain something. Let us suppose that he receives thirty thousand francs; as you may imagine I wish nothing for myself. Emmanuel will return the money that he owes me, be it understood; but I do not wish anything more. Only I have said to him, 'You will make a present to Antonia.' He will give her a necklace that we have bargained for together and that will cost him eight thousand francs. I like better that he should give that, in preference to anything else. Diamonds above all have always an intrinsic value. Afterwards he can pay the upholsterer, the domestics—the dressmaker, and a crowd of little brawling debts which Antonia has made since she has been with him. After that they can live tranquilly with what remains."

I admired the solicitude Madame d'Orimont evinced

in the appropriation of the money she was about to assist Emmanuel in borrowing, but I saw that in this appropriation she did not comprise Emmanuel's personal debts; and, the others discharged, I was convinced that there would not remain for him two hundred francs of the loan he was about to contract.

"Indeed, madame," said I, "it will be a real service that you render to Emmanuel; unhappily, when all you name shall be paid, there will remain nothing for him but his personal debts."

"Oh! that concerns himself. He had no occasion to have contracted them. That which I desire above all is the tranquillity of my girl. Antonia has no fortune, whilst Emmanuel has. It is not she who has asked him to live with her, it is he who has tormented her to do so. The debts which he has made for her are sacred debts, and I will not borrow money for him but on the condition that he will pay them."

"But if Emmanuel's mother hears of this loan and prevents it?"

"Then I myself shall lend the amount to Emmanuel; he will give me an acknowledgment, and you may rest easy that when that is once done, it will be better for the mother to pay: There are the tribunals; and we shall see if Madame de —— would leave the debts of her son to be paid of his mistress."

All this, as you see, was skilfully arranged. There was, therefore, not an instant to be lost in drawing Emmanuel from this new entanglement. I took good care not to let Madame d'Orimont know the purport of my visit. I contented myself with inquiring of her in what hotel she thought Emmanuel would put up at in Havre, adding that I had money to forward to him; this was the best means of learning his address.

"He must be at the Hotel de l'Europe," replied Madame d'Orimont, "in the Rue de Paris."

"Thank you, madame," said I, rising; "I will go and write to him without loss of time." And I took leave of Madame d'Orimont, whom I left before the glass adjusting her collar for the tenth time. The distress of Emmanuel's mother had quite moved me. I had too much at heart the desire that he should leave this horrible life, not to go and seek him and relate to him the result of my visit to his mother, Madame de ——, and my interview with Madame d'Orimont; moreover, I had nothing to do, and I had never seen Havre, so I started. I arrived the next day at the Hotel de l'Europe. Emmanuel's apartment was pointed out to me, for he was living there. I found him breakfasting with Antonia; two young gentlemen friends, whom he had met by accident at Havre, and whom he had invited, were with them, laughing and singing. He uttered an exclamation of astonishment on seeing me enter. Antonia had, as it were, a presentiment that she had an enemy in myself, and she gave me a reception of significant coldness and mistrust.

"You here!" cried Emmanuel; "by what chance is this?"

"I have come to see you," I replied; "I was told you were at Havre, so I am come to Havre."

"And you've done well: get a chair, and draw up to the table."

"I have got to speak to you," I said.

"Very well, you can speak to me after we have breakasted; there will be plenty of time. Devil take it! you must always have your breakfast, you know; you must eat!"

I sat down, and I breakfasted as gaily as possible, for the purpose of not disturbing the merriment of the guests. The breakfast over, I passed with Emmanuel into another chamber.

"I have seen your mother," I said to him.

"Ah! well; she of course inveighed strongly against me?"

"On the contrary, she consents to give you the money you want."

"On what condition?—for she is not a woman not to make one."

"She will pay all your debts, on the condition that you will go and live two or three months in Touraine with her."

"Thank you very much; that's too dear."

"What shall you do then?"

"Why, I have found money, and I shall not want any

of her. After all, my dear fellow, Antonia is a beautiful and good girl, who loves me well, and doesn't cost very much. I have resolved to live quietly with her."

"And your mother, who weeps, who grieves, who waits for you!"

"Eh! well; I will go and see her on my return; but now that I have money, I will not quit Paris for anything in the world."

"What shall I say to Madame de ——?"

"Whatever you like. But listen, now; there's a good thing to be done."

"What is it?"

"Are you of my opinion? I find that one can never have too much money."

"I think exactly as you do."

"Well, then, if I take the fifty thousand francs that my mother offers me, and the thirty thousand that Madame d'Orimont will borrow for me, what should you think of that?"

"I should think that it would be the fourth time that you had deceived your mother; and that in truth, that would be at the least three times too often."

"Ah, my dear fellow! how miserable you are, and how you see things in such a bad light. This is done every day and no murder comes of it."

At this moment Antonia opened the door.

"Emmanuel, will you take any coffee?" said she, appearing to forget that I was there.

"Yes, I will. Come, then," he said to me, "come, let us go back into the other room." And, taking Antonia's head in his two hands, he kissed it repeatedly, and added, turning it towards me, and showing it to me—

"Have you ever seen anything so pretty as that?"

Antonia threw at me a victorious glance, which seemed to say, "I am stronger than you; and all that you may be able to say will do nothing against me."

Evidently Emmanuel, in a weak moment, had owned to her the purport of the visit that I was to have made him in Paris; and in twenty-four hours, by the aid of a promise of money, she had regained all her empire over him. I found my position rather a ridiculous one, so I left Havre the same day; and I did so, I ought to add, without Emmanuel evincing the slightest desire to detain me. I would have laid a wager that he was delighted at my departure. Young gentlemen who live as he was living, do not perceive the error of such existence until they are without funds. Now, I was well convinced that it would not be very long before I had some news of him, for, after the account which Madame d'Orimont had given to me, the new loan, even if she succeeded in raising it, would not last long with the poor fellow.

CHAPTER IV.

A MOTHER'S GRIEF.

I COULD not dispense with a visit to Madame de ——, although it filled me with pain; for I had not a word of good news to take to her. Nevertheless, I went to see her, and I told her a portion of the truth; for I have always remarked, that whatever one may have to relate, the truth, be it what it may, should still have the preference.

"I expected such result," Madame de —— answered, when I had ceased speaking; "nothing astonishes me now on the part of my son."

The sorrow of the poor lady was indeed great; and this, be it remembered, was a grief augmented by fears for the future. I thought to myself, as I left her, that if Emmanuel could see his mother, his heart must indeed be hardened did it turn away from the happiness of appeasing a grief of which it was the cause.

Fresh from this interview, I wrote to him on the subject. He did not reply to me. I determined that I would not visit Mademoiselle Antonia. Experience is the best counsel that can be given to a man. You have a friend foolishly in love, committing all sorts of follies or worse, as in Emmanuel's case, ruining himself for a girl that does not love him in return; for did she love him, she would not leave him to ruin himself. He himself felt that it was not genuine love.

It may be asked why I interfered in this affair? It was the despair of poor Madame de —— that took my heart; also, I must confess, I had ever before my eyes the air of triumph with which Mademoiselle Antonia had greeted me at Havre. I already knew that the Duke de Pololi had been her lover, also the Prince Korloff; but I was convinced that this was not all the history of Mademoiselle Antonia. I learned that Madame d'Orimont had first sold her daughter to the Prince Korloff, she having given herself away six months before to an officer of the cuirassiers; secondly to the Duke de Pololi; to an Englishman; to the son of a banker, and to the director of a theatre. Between these different sales Antonia had as lovers a law student, a pupil of the Polytechnic School, a young "first gentleman" of the Montparnasse theatre, a "second-gentleman" of the Beaumarchais theatre, two provincial directors, and seven unknowns, who had only given their Christian names. I also discovered that Madame d'Orimont enriched herself solely by employing with her daughter's lovers the same proceeding as with Emmanuel, that is to say, she lent them for a third the money she had economised of what they gave to Antonia; thus their own money supplied the loan they took at an exaggerated rate. I learnt that the infant and the pension from the Duke de Pololi was a pure invention of that good Madame d'Orimont.

More infamous than all, it was told to me on all sides she asserted that Emmanuel wished to marry her, but that she did not wish him to do so; adding, that she kept him for charity; indeed, that it was she who maintained him. I learnt, indeed, that she was an ignoble creature, and that Emmanuel was playing the part of a simpleton.

I sat down and wrote a long, earnest letter to Emmanuel, in which I detailed to him all that I had heard. received his reply immediately; it read thus—

"MY DEAR FRIEND—

"I thank you for your counsel, but I never take counsel save from myself. I know not what interest you have to make yourself the echo of all these calumnies. I love and esteem Mademoiselle Antonia; and I do not in future desire to see any but those who will entertain the same sentiments for her that I do myself.

"Your old friend,

"Emmanuel de ——."

I dismissed my friend, Antonia, and Madame d'Orimont to the devil, and no longer troubled myself about them.

Six months had passed, when one morning I walked into a *cafe* on the Boulevard to breakfast. The first person that caught my eye on entering was Emmanuel.

I scarcely knew on what terms we were, nevertheless I went up to him, and offered him my hand, and asked him how he was. He shook hands with me, and replied, apparently with great spirits, that he was wonderfully well. I moved on, as though going to take a seat at a table at the other end of the room.

"But where are you going?" said he.

"I am going to breakfast."

"Well, sit down here, and breakfast with me."

I sat down. I avoided speaking of Antonia, but I thought I saw by Emmanuel's face that he observed my silence on the subject; and, at the same time, I fancied he was desirous that I should refer to it. I conversed upon all topics save that one. We left the place together.

"Adieu!" I said to him.

"You leave me already?" he inquired, gloomily.

"Yes, I must."

"Come and see me, then?"

"Well, I have scarcely the time; I work a good deal."

"However, if you pass the Rue de la Victoire, come up and say good-day to one."

"You live there, then, now?"

"Yes."

Emmanuel evidently waited for some new question on my part; none was made, and we separated.

At the moment that we turned our backs on each

other I found myself face to face with another of my friends, one whom I was less acquainted with than with Emmanuel; his name was Octave, I believe."

"Who were you talking with?" he asked.

"With Emmanuel de ——."

"I was not mistaken, then."

"Do you know him?"

"Yes;" then, hesitatingly, "No."

"You tell me that with a droll tone."

"Do you know him much yourself?"

"Yes."

"Ah!"

That "ah!" could be interpreted into "so much the worse for you."

"Don't at all understand the purport of your remarks, of what you say."

"Oh! I say nothing."

Evident it was that Octave asked to be questioned; he, however, continued—

"Was he not the lover of Antonia, an opera dancer?'

"Yes."

"So it is."

"Why the devil this mysterious air?"

"You often see that M. Emmanuel?"

"Yes."

"Well, then, see him less often. There, that is al you can learn from me."

"What has he done?"

"Well, he has a bad reputation. I have had things told me about him."

"What are they?'

"They say he is entirely maintained by Antonia."

"He?"

"He."

"He who has told you that has lied!" I exclaimed, with warmth.

"My dear fellow, it is a man who knows him better than anybody; it is Antonia's new lover, who now pays the debts of this gentleman, who has said so."

"Listen, my dear Octave; for six months I have not seen Emmanuel, but I will certify to you that there is not a word of truth in that which has been told to you."

"Well, that is not all."

"What else is there?"

"He has been seen to cheat at play."

"He never plays."

"He has played, I tell you, for I have played against him."

"And you have seen him cheat, yourself?"

"No, on the contrary, I have always seen him lose; and he has paid directly."

"Who accuses him, then?"

"It is Antonia's lover who does so."

"Tell me the name of that gentleman."

"It is the Count Ernest de Magny."

"He lives – where?"

"No. 5, Rue de la Paix."

"Thanks."

"What are you going to do with that address?"

"I wish to give it to Emmanuel."

"Oh! give it to him; you can also appeal to my evidence, if needed, and say it was I who told all to you The Count has told me of it twenty times, and ten of my friends will tell you as much."

"Is it long that M. de Magny has been the lover of Antonia?"

"It is about two months. But how is it that you, the friend of Emmanuel, know nothing?"

"He has said nothing to me."

"Not just now."

"No."

"Yet you knew of his love affair?"

"Better than anybody; that is why I can affirm that what M. de Magny has said is a pure calumny; not only Emmanuel was not kept (since the word must be said) by Mademoiselle Antonia, but more, he ruined himself for her."

"All that I know is, that the Count told me so; but I am ignorant as to who told him. Yet he would not have advanced an assertion of this gravity had he not been certain of the fact."

After that I took leave of Octave, and went straight to where Emmanuel lived.

CHAPTER V.

ANTONIA'S EMBARRASSMENT.

I FOUND Emmanuel in a small furnished lodging in the Rue de la Victoire. So modest was the appearance of his dwelling, that I am sure at the most it could not have cost him more than eighty francs a month. I discovered my friend sitting by his fireside, smoking and reading a book.

"My dear fellow," I immediately exclaimed to him, on entering, "I am come to speak to you of something very serious."

"Sit down, my friend," said Emmanuel, taking my hand, "sit down, and tell it to me at once.'

Without prelude, I said—

"You have left Antonia—how was that done?"

"Oh, my dear fellow, I am ashamed to confess it to you," answered Emmanuel, after a momentary pause of hesitation; "and yet I must tell you. At Havre, she had so set me against you, for she guessed rightly the object of your visit, that for fifteen days I really disliked—detested you. We returned to Paris. Every day did I implore Madame d'Orimont to advance the sum she had promised to lend me, for I counted on being able, with that amount, to pay a portion of my private debts. I received thirty thousand francs against a bill of exchange for forty thousand. To tell you how that money went would be impossible. I restored to Madame d'Orimont that which I owed her. I made Antonia a present —I paid what debts I was responsible for on her account —servants, tradesmen, and others; and I then found myself exactly in the same position, face to face with my debts—just as pinched and tormented as before. I have not a sou in the world. I am quite estranged from my mother, and tracked by my creditors. Well, I find myself happy in comparison with what I was when with Antonia."

"But how did you break it off?"

"From the moment that I had paid Antonia's debts I could see that, both on her part and on the part of her mother, there was no longer much consideration on my account. Each day they volunteered to break off their bargain. Each day there perpetually came to my knowledge infamous statements made about me by Antonia. Through recrimination we were continually at variance. My reproaches, when I discovered her deceptions, gained at first but denials; but this finished by her telling me she was indifferent to my opinions and feelings, and that I might go as soon as I liked. I began thenceforth to understand how I had been duped, and I fancied that I was avenging myself by staying. I at last gave myself that reason for remaining; the truth was I had become so habituated to pass my life thus, that I was at a loss to know how otherwise it was to be employed. Yet I did not love her! This lasted for nearly two months. One evening she played; I went out, and did not return until midnight, when I went straight to her apartment. I rang the bell a dozen times, louder and louder each time, but there was no reply. I went down again; the porter at the entrance door of the house was in bed, and I dared not venture to rouse him and inquire from him whether Antonia was at home; it was quite enough to be ridiculous in my own eyes, without also making myself ridiculous in the sight of that man. My self-pride whispered a crowd of improbable reasons for her absence. I waited thus until two o'clock in the morning without seeing her enter. Wandering about till nine o'clock in the morning, then I went to the door again, and loudly rang. This time a servant came and opened the door.

"Is Mademoiselle within?" was my first inquiry.

"No, sir," replied the domestic, with a certain embarrassment; "madame has gone out."

"I will wait for her, then."

"That is impossible, sir."

"Why so? why is it impossible?"

"Madame has taken away all the keys."

The coachman, who had recognised my voice, at this moment came up.

"I have a letter for you, sir."

"From whom?"

" From madame.'

" It seemed to me that the coachman and maid-servant were laughing at me. The former went and found the letter and brought it to me. The letter contained these words—

'My Dear Emmanuel,—

'We are unhappy together; one of us must be more reasonable than the other;—you are not so, I am. Come and see me as a friend, if you will; but all other relation between us must cease. I no longer belong to myself.

'Antonia.'

" 'Very well,' stammered I (for such a dismissal is not received without at least astonishing one); 'very well. Say to your mistress that I must beg her to return to me that which is here belonging to me—at least, unless she intends to steal it from me.' The words were not in very good taste, but so enraged was I with her treatment of me, that it was impossible to restrain their utterance. The same day my effects were returned to me, with an insolent letter, in which she told me, that after speculating upon her, I had so far forgotten myself as to insult her, and were it not that she despised me, she would have sent someone after me that would have brought me back to my senses."

" Since then," said I, " you have never heard Antonia spoken of?"

"On the contrary, every day we hear of her circulating fresh calumnies about me. She has said to each of my creditors that I am a blackguard, and never intended to pay them; and at this hour no reputation in Paris so infamous as mine."

"But that is not all," said I, and then narrated to Emmanuel all the conversation that had passed between myself and Octave.

"This scandal on myself has been well merited," said he; "no one knows the injury that a woman, despicable as she must be, can inflict upon an honourable man, when she is young and pretty, and surrounded by people who pay court to her. Do me the favour to go to the Count de Magny, that all this may terminate with a good duel; that is all he is asked."

The result of our visit, myself and Octave, was that M. de Magny had but to repeat that which Mademoiselle Antonia had told to him, and which, he stated, he could only retract if the lady did the same.

We went to the lady, whom we found supported by her mother. One volume would not suffice to transcribe in all the calumnies these two hussies heaped on Emmanuel. They respected nothing—neither delicacy, nor family, nor honour.

Emmanuel fought with M. de Magny; he gave him a sword wound. He paid all his debts; he sacrificed a portion of his fortune; he went and lived in Touraine with his mother, and broke off completely with a world for which he was not made. This does not prevent there still being found people who, when he is spoken of, say to you—

"Emmanuel de ——, who was the lover of Antonia, was not so upright a fellow as he appeared to be. Very villainous things are related about him."

Some six months ago I met Emmanuel, whom I had not seen for a year past. I naturally spoke to him of Antonia.

"Stay!" he said to me; "you must do me a service."

"What is it?"

"That you go to her, and take her these five hundred francs."

And at the same time he took a five hundred franc-note from his pocket-book.

"You are mad," I said to him. "You yet send money to Antonia?"

"Yes; the poor girl has written to me that she is very unhappy: that they are going to sell her furniture; and that she has positive want of that sum."

"Have you her letter about you?"

"Here it is."

That letter was thus expressed:—

"My Dear Emmanuel,—

"I am exceedingly embarrassed, and must absolutely have five hundred francs to-day. I address myself to you, because of all the gentlemen that I know, you have the most heart, and will be the most prompt to render me this service, in remembrance of the happy time that we have passed together."

I took the five hundred franc-note and went to Antonia's with it.

"I come," said I to her, "on the part of Emmanuel.'

"He has received my letter?" said she to me.

"Yes."

"He has sent to me—"

"Five hundred francs; there they are."

"Oh! how kind he is! You will thank him very much for me. Why has he not come himself? I should have had much pleasure in seeing him."

"That is not, however, what you said to me the last time I saw you; you treated Emmanuel very badly."

"Oh! you know," she remarked, carelessly, "one says things when one is angry, and the next day one regrets having said them."

See how the reputations of young men are made and unmade. Everything I had said to Emmanuel the day of our first interview at Antonia's was realised. Decidedly experience is a fruit that one can never gather but when it is rotten.

Part the Third.

REMINISCENCES OF A PARISIAN MOUCHARD.

REMINISCENCES OF A PARISIAN MOUCHARD.

OVER a shop in one of the best streets of the Faubourg Saint Antoine, there had been for many years painted in large letters, "Jean Baptiste Soult, Ebinste" (cabinet-maker). Such a name so placed naturally excited a good deal of ironical remark, and the cabinet maker had been compelled by authority to prove his right to call himself by so illustrious a name. He did so indisputably; adding, that he was distantly related to the famous Marshal, whose baptismal and sire name he bore.

The cabinet-maker certainly was, like his renowned namesake, an uncompromising Bonapartist, which craze might no doubt have been a blood disease.

Now Jean Baptiste, as for brevity's sake we will call the honest man, was also a Republican of the most exalted kind; confounding, by some incomprehensible mental process, as did Beranger, and hundreds of other gifted men, the ideas of Despotism and of Liberty, the impersonations of Force and Freedom—singular, yet wide-spread delusion!

While Jean Baptiste had given hostages to fortune—a prosperous business, a considerable investment in Rentes, and, above all, his child Josephine, a duteous, most loveable girl, then in the bloom of her seventeenth summer —he, swayed, dominated by his strong predilections, in an evil hour consented, though not, we must suppose, without misgiving, to join a secret society.

One of the members of that society was a Monsieur Le Moine, Auguste Le Moine, a tall, handsomeish man of forty, who, it was evident by his carriage and general bearing, had served in the army. In the ranks it must have been, as he assumed no military title ; yet he was a man of education and refined manners.

The simple minded cabinet-maker highly admired the out-spoken, defiant Imperialist-Republican, invited him to his house, lent him money, introduced him to tailors, and finally invited him to take up his abode altogether with him. Le Moine very gladly consented, and one of the best apartments in the house was fitted up for his use, all which favours he repaid by highly-wrought descriptions of the campaigns of Spain and Portugal, in which his excellent host's "illustrious relative" played so distinguished a part, and with respect to which he pretended to be in possession of exclusive and certainly peculiar information.

There never was a more voracious *gobe-mouche* than honest Jean Baptiste. The quantities of snuff with which upon such occasions the delighted cabinet-maker gratified his nose, the emphatic taps upon the lid of the box marking time to some more than usually audacious bounce, were amusing to behold.

The absorbed, earnest attention with which Josephine listened, was *not* amusing; quite the reverse. Le Moine's Belial tones seemed to have a strangely fascinating power over her. The beams and smiles that usually decked her innocent, girlish face, vanished; she became excited, pale, and there was a troubled, terrified, yet enthusiastic expression in her soft, brown eyes. I feared for Josephine.

Well, this Le Moine—this high flying Imperialist-Republican—was, as the reader will, perhaps, have anticipated, a brother mouchard, in the confidential employ of Louis Philippe's Government!

We were not acting in concert—were, indeed, total strangers to each other. In the Paris Prefecture of Police, there are several distinct departments, each having its own separate, distinct organization. One paramount principle governs them all—that the mouchards attached to one section shall not be known to the mouchards of another section. This stringent rule is based upon the maxim—that it may be sometimes necessary to set a rogue to catch a rogue, and that if rogue No. 1 saw that rogue No. 2 was at his heels, No 1's heels would never be tripped up.

Enough of explanation. I proceed. The reports sent in by M. Le Moine—his real name, I believe, was Sartines, and I was told that he had served with the foreign legion in Africa—the reports, I say, of soi-disant Monsieur Le Moine were ample, and considered by them selves quite satisfactory. But a suspicion—how generated I know not—had fastened upon the official mind of the Prefet, that Monsieur Le Moine was an active and skilful agent of the Bonaparte faction—that his loud, eloquent, bold advocacy of Imperialist-Republicanism, assumed, as he pretended, to mask his devoted loyalty to the citizen-king's government. Le Moine's known antecedents strengthened the suspicion reluctantly made.

Well, it being thoroughly understood that I, Theodore Duhamel, with fifty mouchard aliases, was of no politics whatever, it occurred to the "Autorites" at the Prefecture, who had charge of Le Moine, that I was just the person to watch that dubious gentleman, and report truly of his doings as far as I could discover them.

This was at the time of the "Banquets"—precious safety-valves for letting off, with more or less of noise and smoke, the pent-up discontent of the country, which M. Guizot's Government was so mad as to prohibit. The public mind was stirred to its profoundest depths—the apprehension of an imminent and terrible crisis universal. Many causes concurred to produce that agitation, to excite that alarm; the supercilious refusal of any extension of the electoral suffrage, so ridiculously circumscribed—about eighty thousand electors for all France—the venomous activity of the secret societies; and not the least potent ingredients in the seething cauldron were the horrible murder of his wife by the Duc de Praslin, awakening in the French heart its instinctive tiger-hatred of "la noblesse," and the conviction of a Minister of State of the grossest peculation.

Yes, signs of the coming tempest were visible to the dullest eyes. But in the presence of the tremendous peril, the shadow of which fell darker and darker with every passing hour over Paris, the Monarch and Ministry could devise no more eff ctive *paratonnere* than the vigilance of a political police, supported by the bayoncts of a disaffected Bonapartist soldiery!

It will be readily understood that under such circumstances my instructions would be of the most stringent kind. M. Le Moine, there could be little doubt, was a traitor to the Monarchy of July, and he was known to stand highly in the estimation of the conspirators. I was commanded to keep incessant watch over his movements, to dog his steps, furnish a list of his associates, and if there appeared a chance of any advantage accruing therefrom, to favour him with a domiciliary visit, and seize his correspondence.

To have such a gentleman as Auguste Le Moine placed at one's discretion, with the understanding that energetic action, serviceable to the Government, must be initiated without delay by the custodian, was an embarrassing affair. It was, moreover, a task difficult to set about. To obtain a lodgment under the same roof with Le Moine was my first consideration. I stumbled at that first step. Jean Baptiste Soult had no lodging-room in his house for M. Abatucci, of Corsican parentage, but born and educated in France, whose father, a chevalier of the Legion of Honour, had fallen at Waterloo, absolutely under the eye of the great Emperor. The excellent Jean was extremely sorry, desolated, that he could not find accommodation in his house for so distinguished a gentleman as M. Abatucci; but positively he could not; and the tradesman whose name I could not recollect, if he had been any time in the neighbourhood, should have known that he, Jean Baptiste Soult—

"Ah, yes; and a relative, I have been told, of the great Marshal?"

"It is true—distantly related to the illustrious Marshal—the tradesman should have known, I was saying, that Jean Baptiste Soult did not habitually let any of his apartments. In parting, he begged to express a hope that M. Abatucci, whenever passing that way, would honour him with a call."

This check was soon partially remedied. Nearly opposite Soult's establishment was a private house, in one of the windows of which was a printed bill announcing "Chambres garnies a louer" (furnished rooms to let). One of these, a front apartment, I engaged, and took possession of the same day.

I could now watch M. Le Moine's movements, myself unseen, unsuspected, and I could improve my acquaintance with Jean Baptiste Soult. That knowledge, as to when Le Moine went out, and came back, I mean, might have results.

The house was kept by a widow, Madame Tussaud, who boasted that she was a cousin, several degrees removed, of the Madame Tussaud who had made, or was making, an immense fortune in London by the exhibition of wax figures.

That may or may not have been true. I believe it was true, because I found her to be generally a truthful person.

Well, I was now in possession of an observatory from which I could watch the exits and entrances of M. Le Moine. Such a position, utilised by a zealous cultivation of Jean Baptiste's friendship, might suffice to enable me to successfully carry out the instructions of my superiors at the Prefecture.

Le Moine went out every day at about noon, and remained away till five, when he returned to dine with Jean Baptiste and Josephine, who out of compliment to their distinguished guest—he was related, bless you, to half the Napoleonic nobility—had substituted the aristocratic five for the bourgeoise one o'clock dinner hour.

From twelve to five were valuable hours to me. Jean Baptiste was then busy in his workshops at the back of his premises, Josephine confined to the shop. An ardent admirer of books, I had gratefully availed myself of Jean Baptiste's invitation to peruse, in a small back room on the first floor, a choice collection of Bonapartist books.

This gave me the range of the first floor, the only occupied portion of which was Le Moine's apartment. It was not difficult to procure keys that would open the door of the room and the desk in which he kept his papers. I was thus enabled to take copies of Le Moine's letters at leisure, and which copies were duly forwarded by post to the Prefecture.

Several of the letters had an interest, other than political for me. They were from Le Moine's wife, who was living with their children at Rheims. They were requests for money—little else. Evidently Le Moine was not an esteemed, beloved, or loving husband. That was no concern of mine; but it did concern me to let Jean Baptiste know that his confidential, trusted bachelor friend, Le Moine, who was paying such earnest if indirect courtship to susceptible Josephine, was a married man with a large family.

Eugene Dubarle, a medical student, had, previous to the advent of Le Moine, been a frequent and welcome visitor at Jean Baptiste's house, the attraction being to him, without question, Josephine. He had found favour, I understood, with the damsel, and personally with her father. Dubarle, when roused, was hot and bitter of speech, and on one occasion, myself being present, stung by the sarcastic comments of Le Moine, aimed with civilly-toned, but venomous virulence at him, and graciously received, smiled at by Josephine, he launched out with a fierce, passionate invective, against the Corsican Brigand, as he chose to designate Napoleon le Grand.

Uproar! Tempest! Fierce exclamation! Jean Baptiste, mildest of men, was enraged beyond measure—Josephine indignant; the scene terminating by a stern intimation from the outraged Jean, that he should for the future decline the honour of M. Dubarle's acquaintance. The fiery young man rejoined that he desired nothing better, went off in unmitigated rage, and Le Moine more than ever was master of the situation.

Now I was strongly of opinion that dazzled, fascinated, carried off her feet, as Mademoiselle Soult evidently was by the seductive homage of a practised roue, she still felt a real preference for Eugene Dubarle. Acting upon that opinion, I penned an anonymous letter to the hastily-discarded lover, informing him that M. Le Moine, who, the writer had heard, was the rival of his for a certain young lady's favour, was a married man, the father of a family, and that the wife's address was No. 15, Rue des Capuchins, Rheims.

This note I posted before breakfast, and on the very same day Eugene Dubarle presented himself at Jean Baptiste's for the first time since the quarrel. He apologised to Jean Baptiste, bowed somewhat proudly to Josephine, and seated himself without being asked. The situation was an embarrassing one for all present. Jean Baptiste, who had, mechanically, as one may say, accepted the young man's proffered hand, snuffed prodigiously, Josephine crimsoned with blushes, looked anywhere but in the direction of the new comer, with whom Le Moine exchanged haughty, defiant glances. Presently, recovering his scarcely ruffled nonchalance, Le Moine resumed the topic upon which he had been dilating—the eternal one of Napoleon and " your illustrious relative's " glorification—when of a sudden thunder fell in the midst.

" Is it your opinion, M. le Moine," interrupted Dubarle, " that in the event of the French nation recovering, as you phrase it, the thread of its true destiny, by raising again the popular throne of the Napoleons, the hero of Strasburg would elect to be crowned, as our old line of monarchs were, at Rheims ?"

" At Rheims ! What can it signify to me or to you where a Napoleon may elect to be crowned ?" said Le Moine, startled by the bitter irony of Dubarle's tone, and the peculiar emphasis he had placed upon " Rheims."

" Yes, Rheims," continued Dubarle, " where your wife, Madame Le Moine, and children are living ; and not in a very prosperous condition, I am told."

" What—what did you say ?" stammered M. Le Moine, starting up from his cha r.

Jean Baptiste and his daughter had also risen, and both stood gazing alternately from Le Moine to Dubarle—from Dubarle to Le Moine.

" I said that your wife and children reside at Rheims, in a not too prosperous condition."

" Liar !" shouted Le Moine, in a furious voice, white with rage and dismay. " Liar !"

" This is not the fitting place for requiting, as it deserves," retorted Dubarle, with exultant bitterness, "but a fitting time and place will present themselves, never fear!"

Just then the door of the apartment was flung open, and five or six Sergen de Ville entered. They had come to arrest Le Moine, accused of conspiring with others against the Government, and his immediate destination was the prison Mazas.

"Liar! Coward! Scoundrel!" he exclaimed, addressing Dubarle, "I owe this to you!"

"That is false! I did not imagine you had sufficient courage to conspire against a state."

"Liar! A liar always!" hoarsely shouted Le Moine, whilst madly struggling with the Sergen de Ville. "Liar! a liar always!"

Presently recognising the insanity of resistance, he resigned himself to destiny, and was led off.

He was gone, and when I looked round, Josephine had disappeared. All the ardent sympathies, and the prejudices of the cabinet-maker were called into play by the arrest of his friend, at, he firmly believed, the instigation of Dubarle. He presume to the favour of Josephine Soult! He would himself rather see his child the wife of the poorest man in Paris, than the bride of Dubarle. The scene terminated by Dubarle's exit in a towering rage, but not till he, in his turn, had flung scathing words of defiance, scorn, and contempt in the face of Jean Baptiste Soult.

I need hardly say that it was the transcripts of his letters, forwarded to the Prefecture by unsuspected M. Abatucci, that had really caused the arrest of Le Moine. Yes, and a good result had been arrived at, for the latter was imprisoned, and prevented from prosecuting his machinations against the peace and honour of the Soult family.

My mission, as regarded Le Moine, was accomplished, and I gave up my domicile at Madame Tussaud's. I also took quiet, friendly leave, of Jean Baptiste. His daughter I did not see after the abusive expulsion of Dubarle till the hour of the catastrophe of this drama had struck.

. . . . .

After this I was employed in inquiries amongst the widowed Duchesse D'Orleans' household with respect to the mysterious disappearance of a number of valuable jewels from a casket in the boudoir of her Royal Highness. I was still engaged in that duty on the third day of the revolt against the prohibition of the great "Banquet," when the triumph of the Insurrection being no longer doubtful, that heroic princess, taking counsel only of her courage, determined to present herself with her children before the Chamber of Deputies, in assertion of her own and their right.

I, with, I think, all the male members of the household, pressed after that queenly woman, entered the chamber close after her, and found myself, as she did, amidst a crowd of shouting ruffians.

As the Duchess and her children were being hurried out of the hall, a strong grasp was placed upon my arm! Turning round, I found myself face to face with Madame Tussaud.

"I have found you at last!" she said, in a hurried whisper; "Poor Josephine Soult has been carried off by brutal force. Taking advantage of the anarchy which everywhere prevails, three or four brigands, hired, it is known, by Dubarle, have committed the abominable outrage."

"Dubarle!" said I, as yielding to the woman's impulse, I pressed with her through the clamorous crowd, "Dubarle! It is impossible!"

"It is true, nevertheless. The brigands admitted, in the hearing of the servant, Lisette, that they were employed by Dubarle."

"Proof positive to my mind, that they were *not* employed by Dubarle. Unfortunate Josephine!"

"Jean Baptiste Soult," continued Madame Tussaud, "was brought home wounded in the head by a sabre-stroke about an hour after his child had been carried off. The terrible tidings which awaited him smote the bereaved father to the ground. He has not spoken since. The revolutionists have much to answer for."

. . . . .

Lisette Hamon's tale was soon told. She and Josephine had sat up all night anxiously awaiting the return home of Jean Baptiste, who had been absent since about noon the previous day. Towards morning, but long be fore it was light, there was a loud knocking at the street-door. Believing it was Jean Baptiste who demanded ad-mittance, daughter and servant both hastened to the door, which was no sooner opened, than in rushed three men—who seized, and in a twinkling effectually gagged the astounded women. Josephine was driven off in a fiacre. "Present M. Dubarle's compliments to le Coquin Rouge, your master," said the leading ruffian, "and tell him that it is thus that Henri-Cinquist Dubarle re-quites the insults of a Bonapartist Jacobin!"

"A shallow subterfuge," said I. "Dubarle has had as much to do with the abduction as myself."

"Monsieur Le Moine—"

"When did you see him last?"

"He is with Baptiste Soult at this moment."

"Hundred devils! Conduct me, if you please, to Jean Baptiste Soult."

Poor Soult was lying in a state of partial paralysis—loss of speech chiefly. Le Moine had gone away a few moments before I entered the sick chamber. I sought to comfort the afflicted father by predicting that I should soon recover his child. The strong pressure of my hand, the quick suffusion of his eyes thanked me, and I left.

Dubarle was not at his lodgings, had not been there during the previous twenty-four hours. What might that mean? The faith I had in his honour and rectitude was rudely shaken.

I was completely at fault. The inquiries I made that day, the next, and the next, led to nothing. Le Moine, in high favour with the Provisional Government, could not be questioned, least of all by me, whose vocation and real name had, I found, been made known to him by the new Prefect of Police. I despaired of the unhappy Josephine, prisoned in the clutch, I could hardly doubt, of that consummate conspirator and scoundrel.

Still, what had become of Dubarle? Had he fallen in one of the street fights?

A letter addressed to Signor Abatucci, at Madame Tussaud's, apprised me that he was temporarily resting at a cottage near Fougeres, and that he was very desirous of seeing me without delay. There were interests of deepest moment, which he was anxious to place under my charge. Not one word of Josephine Soult!

I thoughtlessly showed the letter to M. Tussaud. She at once came to the conclusion that it was indeed Dubarle who had carried off Josephine, and who, already weary of his prize, wished to consult me as to the best plan, in his own interest, well understood, of getting rid of the ruined girl. Such a conclusion was too absurd for serious reflection, and simply remarking that I should set off at once for Fougeres, I bade the rashly-judging woman adieu.

Within an hour afterwards, Lisette Hamon believed

with her that the triumphant ravisher was Dubarle, which belief, together with the name of the place where his daughter and her betrayer might be found, were communicated to and impressed upon the excited brain of Jean Baptiste himself, by Lisette Hamon, before the day was two hours older. Jean Baptiste had, it is necessary to observe, recovered from the attack of paralysis, and though still weak and feverish, had been authoritatively pronounced to be convalescent.

It was a smart half-hour's walk from Fougeres to Monsieur Deslan es' cottage. Madame Desladdes was within, but her husband and Dubarle had gone out together, and she did not expect their return in less than two hours. "If I was the person whom Dubarle expected from Paris," added the good woman, "I should be glad to hear that the young lady, whose civil marriage had taken place that morning at Fougeres—"

"Married! married this morning! Not till th's morn ing; and it is ten days since Josephine was brutally seized and carried off! It is an infamy, permit me to say, of which I could not have believed Dubarle would have been guilty. Yes, an infamy: and not the less so, because Mademoiselle Soult has found herself compelled to condone the outrage. Can I speak with the bride?"

"She is unwell, and just now asleep. When she awakes you can speak with her. And permit *me* to observe," cont nued Madame Deslandes, in a grave and somewhat bi:ter tone—"that Monsieur Dubarle, who I have known from infancy—he is my foster-son – will never be justly accused of a bad action. Chargeable with folly he may be, is, in my opinion, so chargeable, in this unhappy affair. Be seated, Monsieur," added the good lady. "Dubarle is anxious that you should be the interpreter with the young lady's father, who—"

"To be sure—to be sure," I interrupted, with heat. "Having first possessed himself of the lady, he is next desirous of securing the dowry."

"Once again, you are mistaken. Dubarle does not covet, will not, be assured, accept a faithing of the old man's money.

"To do so would be to degrade the sacrifice—the painful, cruel sacrifice, according to me—which Dubarle, under the influence of a credulous, romantic tenderness, has made into a vile money speculation. You do not know my foster-son, Monsieur. He may be poor in a positive sense, but he is proud, independent, as the richest man in France—the pride, the independence of honour, I mean. After hearing what I have to say, you will estimate him more justly, and I shall speak with entire frankness."

The warm-hearted woman did speak with entire frankness, and at great length. I must epitomise the narrative.

Josephine Soult, dragged from her father's house by ruffians hired by Le Moine, was conveyed to a house of shame in Par s, and kept a close prisoner there for seven days. The outrage was prompted—Madame Deslandes suggested, therein echoing Dubarle's opinion,—was prompted less by illicit passion for Josephine, than by a fierce determination to be aveuged upon Dubarle, to whom he attributed his arrest, and who he knew was devotedly attached to Josephine. During five of those seven days Dubarle was staying with the Deslandes. He had sought shelter with them till the Saturnalia in the capital should have subsided. Order restored, he had gone back to Paris, and returned the very next day, bringing with him Josephine, h s civil marriage with whom had taken place that morning. On the morrow the blessing of the church would be given to the union, which, accomplished, it was not doubted that Jean Baptiste, informed through me of all the circumstances, would accept.

This was the substance of the story, as told by Ma 'ame Des'andes by Dubarle, the exact verity of which I had neither the means nor inclination to rigorously test. Madame Deslandes evidently believed that her foster-son had, under the influence of a too generous tenderness sacrificed himself to save the reputation of Josephine. I fully coincided with that opinion, till I found that Dubarle's faith in his bride's stainless purity was unclouded by a doubt: and that, after closely observing Josephine herself, I saw that, pale and weak as she was, not the faintest shadow of deceit dimmed the clear candour of a face of which that expression had always been the principal charm.

I readily undertook to see and explain matters to Jean Baptiste Soult, and everything having been said that it was deemed desirable to say, I was about to depart for Paris. We, Monsieur Deslandes and I, the evening being fine and warm for the season of the year, had been taking wine in his large, finely-cultivated garden, the back gate of which chanced to be wide open. The lover and his bride, he with his arm round Josephine's waist, were seated in a kind of rustic chair longue, not ten paces from the open gate, to which my back, as I shook hands with Deslandes, was for the moment turned. Suddenly, the sharp crack of a pistol shot, followed by piercing screams, rang through the air. Jean Baptiste Soult had entered, unobserved, through the garden-gate, saw, as he believed, his lost child clasped by the arm of her seducer —that seducer the hated Dubarle; and, without a word of warning, in a transport of delirious rage, shot the young man through the back. The screams were Josephine's.

. . .

The wound did not prove fatal, though a long period of suffering elapsed before Dubarle was out of danger, during which time Josephine did not minister to her husband with tenderer solicitude than did Jean Baptiste himself. I should explain that it was given out, that Dubarle had been wounded by accident, and no suspicion to the contrary having arisen, a legal inquiry had not been instituted.

Meanwhile Jean Baptiste had sold his business and removed to a house belonging to him in the Boulevard du Temple. He was a changed man ; had become silent, reserved, and rarely discussed politics. From Dubarle he had exacted a solemn pledge never, should he chance to meet with Le Moine, to show any resentment, or make the slightest allusion to the outrage upon Josephine. He himself avoided all mention of the subject, except to me. Thus whilst Josephine and her husband believed he had dismissed the hateful subject from his mind, *I* knew that he was constantly brooding over it—meditating how he could avenge the dishonour of his daughter without bringing public scandal upon her name, which in the general ear had not been associated with that of Le Moine, who, for his own sake, had kept strict silence on the matter. Though always the doting father, Jean Baptiste was not, like Dubarle, just to Josephine ; and nothing, it was plain, could shake the gloomy conviction that had settled upon his mind, and was festering at his heart.

. . . . .

A considerable time passed before Jean Baptiste was offered a chance of gratifying his burning thirst for vengeance. Le Moine, appointed one of the Commissioners for preaching up, in doubtful departments, the excellence of the actual government, with the object of securing the election of thorough going republican candidates for seats in the Assembly, had left Paris on his mission. He remained several months absent, and after he returned, Jean Baptiste found it difficult to meet with him, and impossible for a long while, when he chanced to do so at a restaurant, to fasten a legitimate quarrel upon him.

An opportunity eagerly seized, at last occurred at the Freres Provencaux, where both dined in near proximity with each other. A hot political dispute arose between Le Moine and one of his companions, which Jean Baptiste found a pretext for joining in. Not having been present, I cannot state the precise particulars; bnt I understood that the quarrel was initiated by an assertion by Jean Baptiste, that Le Moine, who declaimed so gravely against Kings—against Royalism of every shade, had himself been a paid active mouchard agent of Louis Philippe's Government. Le Moine retorted by an angry denial. Jean Baptiste, desiring nothing better than that, flung back the denial in his enemy's teeth; adding that he had not only been a Louis Philippe's mouchard, but was actually a liar and a rascal! A glass of wine flung in his face was Le Moine's rejoinder, and Baptiste's game was made. It was settled there should be a meeting in the Bois de Boulogne, in precisely two hours from that time.

Jean Baptiste drove from the place direct to my lodgings, and requested me to act as his second in the duel about to take place. For several reasons I positively declined the honour, and suggested that Sous-Lieutenant

Gaspard, an acquaintance of mine, and an expert in such affairs, would, I had no doubt, undertake the required duty. I knew where at that time of day to meet with Gaspard, who at once acceded to our joint request.

His cheerful countenance fell when I named my friend's antagonist.

"Diable !—Auguste Le Moine ! You could not have selected a more dangerous customer in all Paris. His skill in the use of both sword and pistol is something wonderful, and he has nerves of iron. Are you well practised, Monsieur Soult, in the use of either weapon?" he added.

Jean Baptiste was compelled to confess that he was not well practised in the use of either sword or pistol. He should take his chance nevertheless.

"A pretty chance !" exclaimed Gaspard. "I must consider how I can manage to give you a chance with Le Moine. Let me see—let me see. You must pledge me your word of honour," he resumed, after brief reflection, "you must pledge your word of honour that you will fight this duel with the weapon and after the fashion I mean to propose, or not at all?"

Jean Baptiste readily gave the requited word of honour, and would at that moment, it struck me, have preferred, had he a choice, the "not at all" alternative.

"Bon !" said Gaspard. "And now let us have some wine. We have quite an hour to spare."

The grave concern manifested by Gaspard, who was a

good hearted fellow, spite of his predilection for deadly duels, deepened as the time for setting out drew near. Again he suggested that the encounter might perhaps be avoided with honour. Mutual apologies, for example—

Jean Baptiste, whose momently-shaken nerves the wine had restrung, answered that the duel could not, should not, be avoided. He trusted in Lieutenant Gaspard's assurance that, notwithstanding Le Moine's skill as a duelist, he, Soult, should have an equal chance of killing as of being killed.

"It is just: and I undertake either that there shall be no duel, or that the chances shall be equal. A fearful chance for each of you. Your affairs, in case of accident, will be found all arranged?" he added. "That is well; and now we will enjoy our wine."

. . . . .

"I hope you will go with us," said Jean Baptiste, apart to me in a tremulous tone. "Not to take any active part in the affair, but that in case of—of accident, the intelligence may as tenderly as possible be broken to poor Josephine."

It was impossible to refuse such a request. I felt, indeed—and the reflection was a painful one—that I, with the best intentions, had been the primary cause of the catastrophe about to be consummated in the Bois de Boulogne. But for the information relative to Le Moine's wife and family, obtained in my detective capacity, and rashly communicated to Dubarle—his bitter quarrel with Le Moine, and the abduction of Josephine, would never, in all probability, have taken place!"

. . . . .

Le Moine and his second were at the selected rendezvous before us. "Le Capitaine Duval," exclaimed Sous-Lieutenant Gaspard, directly he saw who Le Moine's friend was, "that is fortunate."

"You have the choice of weapons," said Captain Laval, after an interchange of cold civilities. "Which do you choose?"

"Pistols," replied Gaspard.

"Very well; let us load them."

"One moment, Captain Laval!" said Gaspard. "My friend here, Monsieur Jean Baptiste Soult, who is totally unskilled in the use of either pistol or sword, will not have the slightest chance with your friend Le Moine. It will be a murder not a duel."

"I do not comprehend," said Laval. "What do you propose, or why are you here?"

"I propose that the chances shall be made equal for both combatants."

"How are the chances to be made equal?" asked Laval.

"Nothing more easy. You and I, Captain Laval, take

these pistols. We load one, and do not load the other Both then shall be placed in a hat; the duellists will toss for first choice, and possessed of the weapons, shall stand close together, the muzzles of the pistols pressed against their foreheads. We give the signal; the triggers are pulled, crack!—the head of one is blown off—the other stands erect, unharmed. Nothing can be more fair, more just," added Gaspard, with a laughing sneer. "Monsieur Auguste Le Moine, whom I know to be a devoutly pious person—I have myself frequently seen him in a state of edification at the Madeline—will, I am sure, willingly accept a mode of arbitrement which is in fact an invocation of the justice of God."

Le Moine and Laval stared at each other—at Gaspard, in blank, bewildered astonishment.

"Can you be serious?" asked Laval.

"Serious as death. There is, you must remember, a precedent for the proposal. M. Le Moine has, consequently, he being the challenger—"

"Yes; technically."

"M. Le Moine being the challenger, has no option but to accept a proposal which gives him an equal chance with the person he has challenged to mortal combat—unless he chooses to tender an apology."

"No—no—no apology!" exclaimed Jean Baptiste, of whom at sight of Le Moine the demon of vengeance had again taken full possession.

"A retired cabinet-maker will receive no apology from

me," said Le Moine. "The alternative proposition is absurd, outrageous. Nevertheless, I place the affair unreservedly in your hands, Captain Laval."

"Monsieur Soult's social position you knew, and should have remembered, before you assaulted him," said Captain Laval. "As Captain Gaspard remarks," he added, "there is a precedent for this mode of duel· I consent, therefore, on your behalf."

"Quick, then! let us have done with it," cried Le Moine. "I am generally fortunate at games of hazard," he added.

"That is quite true," remarked Gaspard, between whom and Le Moine there was evidently a bitter feud. "That is quite tiue; but loaded dice and loaded pistols are different kinds of playthings."

He then, with Captain Laval, went aside to make preparations for the duel. That was soon done. The manner of presenting the pistols to the combatants was varied at Laval's suggestion. Both were capped, one loaded; the captain approached with one in each hand, holding by the end of the barrels, with the butts presented, first to Le Moine, who won the toss for choice—as if there could be any choice in the matter. The Captain had insisted, in order to prevent the possibility of suspicion, that he himself should not know which was the loaded pistol.

It was a fearful moment when the duellists were placed so near each other that the muzzles of the cocked pistols were within an inch of their foreheads, and their forefingers touched the hair-triggers. Le Moine's self-command was wonderful. True, he was deadly pale, but otherwise impassive as a statue. Jean Baptiste was not so cool, so steady, composed. He had trembled visibly, but he did not for a moment, as one could see by his sternly-compressed lips and flashing eyes, falter in resolution. His illustrious namesake could hardly have behaved better under the circumstances.

" Listen, Messieurs," said le Capitaine Laval. " I shall call out distinctly, one—two—three, pausing half a minute between each number. This Lieutenant Gaspard and I have agreed shall be done, in order to give either of you the option of avoiding this extraordinary duel by the tender of an apology."

" Attention, Messieurs. One—two !" There was considerably more than half a minute's pause, but no sign of yielding being given by either of the men, the fearful " Three " was reluctantly uttered by the captain, instantly followed by a sharp, single report. Le Moine's good fortune at games of chance had deserted him ! His head had been blown to pieces !

Jean Baptiste was erect, wildly staring at the corpse, and, the sustaining excitement passed away, would himself have fallen had I not seized and upheld him by the arm:

" The game is played out," said Captain Laval. " Let us begone. You, Duhamel, will, I suppose, give notice to the authorities of what has occurred, and all other particulars.''

"I undertook to do so: and Jean Baptiste, Sous-Lieutenant Gaspard, and Captain Laval left then and there for Paris.

I have but one word to add—an instructive one. Jean Baptiste Soult never recovered the nervous shock inflicted by that terrible duel. He died at Charenton before the grass had grown on Le Moine's grave.

• • • •

THE Paris insurrection of June, so mercilessly crushed by General Cavaignac, was followed by the wholesale deportation, without trial, not only of the actual Red insurgents, but of many who were simply "suspects," and of a few who were "suspects d'etre suspects" (suspected of being suspicious persons), to the regions of Cayenne and Africa. Permit me to observe that deportation, without trial, from France to unhealthy colonies is not an invention of the second Empire. The honour of that invention belongs of right, like that of passports, to the influential heroes of the French revolution. Napoleon the First adopted and liberally availed himself of it; the republic under Cavaignac did the same; and to Napoleon the Third only belongs the modest merit of having extended, systematised, elevated the exceptional invention to the dignity of a permanent Bonapartean institution.

A but slight feather, comparatively, in the gorgeous plumage of the imperial cap, but one there can be no question which the "Saviour of France" is fairly entitled to wear.

The triumph of General Cavaignac had other results than the overthrow of the Lamartine gimcrack government—one, videlicet—my own rehabilitation as a well trusted mouchard, in confidential communication with the police Prefecture.

Since that cursed duel, I had been under a cloud. Not because duelling is, or ever was, a legal or moral crime in France, but that Le Moine was the favoured friend of a very influential gentleman attached to the Prefecture. That influential gentleman was extinguished accidentally by Cavaignac's cannon; his successor in office happened to be a friend of mine, and Theodore Duhamel had soon money in both pockets again.

Very soon. The blood shed in the streets, alleys, and churches of Paris had not yet dried into the ground, when a note from the newly-promoted friend of mine was placed in my hands. It briefly announced that I had been named to Monsieur Blondel, the millionaire, as a person who would render him efficient service in an affair he was deeply interested in. My official friend added, that immediately after hearing and accurately noting Monsieur Blondel's facts and directions, I was to present myself at the Prefecture, where I should receive the instructions by which I was to be really guided in conducting the important affair with the management of which I was about to be entrusted. Monsieur Blondel would probably call upon me in about an hour after I should have received the note.

There was added in red ink, and in the actual writing of my official friend—" Beaucup depend, Duhamel, de cette affaire que je te confie en pleine confiance que tu y donneras tout ton energie, tout ton zele; comprenez bien que tu auras a compter avec moi, pas avec, Monsieur Blondel"

Thus translated :—

" Much depends, Duhamel, upon this affair, which I confide to thee in full confidence that thou wilt bestow upon it all thy energy, all thy zeal. Understand well that thou wilt have to reckon with me, not with Monsieur Blondel."

. . . .

Monsieur Blondel—I rebaptize a well-known gentleman by that name—Monsieur Blondel, one of the magnates, it would be scarcely an exaggeration to say *the* magnate of the Bourse, was with me considerably within an hour after I received the note from the Prefecture. A lofty personage, who from the height of his golden stilts looked down upon common mortals with a magnificent disdain, awkwardly imitative of the Faubourg Saint Germain.

(The genus Blondel is not confined to Paris; I have myself seen some splendid specimens in London.)

"I am informed," began the magnificent man, after condescendingly seating himself upon a chair, quite unworthy of the honour, and perusing my face through his gold-rimmed eyeglasses, as if I were a promissory note he was asked to discount—"I am informed that you may be useful to me—that you are intelligent; and when in the employ of a well-paying patron, persevering—zealous?"

"I am dumb as to intelligence, monsieur; but persevering zeal in the service of a bountiful patron I can answer for."

"We shall see. You have heard of my son—of Monsieur Achilles Blondel?"

I was obliged to confess that I had not heard of M. Achilles Blondel. The father was, I need not say, world-known, but his son, Achilles, had not yet, within the scope of my limited vision, appeared above the horizon of the universe. Something at least to that effect I said. Nothing could be, I knew, too gross for the fat, fatuous self-esteem of the parvenu millionaire.

"Well, then, I have first to say that Monsieur Achilles Blondel, my son, is going full speed to destruction—to the devil!"

"Ah! Yes, I comprehend; Rouge et Noir—Roulette—"

"You do *not* comprehend. Rouge et Blanc would

be nearer the mark. The infatuated simpleton has been caught in the meshes of an actress. Persists that he will marry her!"

"Dam! That is serious. How will my services avail in such a case?"

"I will tell you. I purchased a chateau soon after the Northern Railway was completed, near Amiens. Not far from us was the modest domicile of a Madame Villebois, widow, and her daughter Estelle—a charming girl, I have never disputed that.

"Madame Villebois, the relict of a captain in the merchant sea service, vegetated with Estelle upon an annuity of about one thousand francs. Estelle was, nevertheless, well enough educated. She had, I was told, fine natural talents.

"One need not say that an ambitious mother, and an artful girl with a pretty face, would, opportunity occurring, seek to entrap and secure a rich young husband. The opportunity occurred. Achilles, who is as inflammable as tinder, fell in love, as the phrase goes, with the charming Estelle, and sacre bleu, would have married the pretty pauper, had I not interposed a peremptory veto.

"Imagine such a folly—such a crime! And, thousand thunders, this 'Varietes' affair is still worse! Still Achilles—an only child, and now made independent of me by a fortune derived from his mother's maiden sister, recently deceased—still Achilles, I say, is not yet irretrievably entrapped. ruined, lost! Chemists, I have heard, can neutralise one deadly poison by another. I propose to imitate the chemists. You follow me?"

"Yes, Monsieur; but blindly as yet."

"You will see plainly enough presently. Estelle Villebois, frenzied by failing to secure the rich prize she had so skilfully angled for—in consequence she was made, as I managed, to believe of her lover's fickleness, threw herself into a river, but was rescued, and is now, I have been informed, a 'fille de joie,' resident in Paris."

"A terrible fate, poor girl."

"Yes, a terrible fate, as you say. Achilles, upon the authority of a letter which I contrived to have posted at Amiens—a bitterly reproachful one, pretendedly dictated by the girl's mother—has no doubt that Estelle perished in the river. He was frantic for a time, and has never been quite himself since. He has contracted, I grieve to say, dissipated, drinking habits; and I have no doubt that his present craze about the 'Varietes' lady, a Mademoiselle Alix, has been caused and is alimented by her likeness—a really striking one—to Estelle Villebois. You begin to perceive a little how your intelligence and zeal, your knowledge of Paris, may be serviceable to me?"

"Not in the least, Monsieur Blondel. Your son and only child, independent of his father, has, goaded by regretful remorse, no doubt, for the supposed death of one Estelle Villebois, fallen into dissipated, drinking habits; is about to marry an actress, because this actress is a striking likeness of the said Estelle Villebois—who now, you are informed, is a 'fille de joie' in Paris. Excuse me, Monsieur, but que le diable m' emporte, if I understand how a detective police-cfficer can help in such an embroglio."

"In this way. I cannot find the said Estelle Villebois She has no doubt changed her name. I am, however, acquainted with several circumstances regarding her, which diligently worked out by an active officer, familiar with Paris, might lead to the discovery of the girl. She cannot have been in Paris more than three months. In that time she would not be much changed in appearance. Here is her portrait."

"A beautiful star-lit face, irradiated with the glory o an ineffable joy; as she looked, no doubt, when the lover first whispered his love."

"I told you Estelle Villebois was a charming girl," said Monsieur le Millionaire. "A striking face," he added, "which you would be sure to recognise."

"Not after the beautiful unfortunate has been exposed to the seven times heated furnace of the Paris papers! This divine painting will long before this have been effaced by the devil's searing irons. But if I should meet with and recognise her—what then?"

"Your intelligence, Monsieur Mouchard," said the great man, with some temper, "does not advantageously display itself to day. Achilles Blondel, my son, could not *now*, by possibility, marry Estelle Villebois. True; but Estelle Villebois, fallen as she is, will have influence enough to extricate Achilles from the clutches of Mademoiselle Alix."

"I understand now. That is not, however, the kind of commission which the note I received from the Prefecture led me to anticipate."

Monsieur Blondel, in reply, observed that the simple duty of subordinate servants of the state was to carry out the orders of their superiors, without questioning whether they were or were not the fittest agents for accomplishing the particular service required of them. In the actual case it could not be doubted, supposing the praise he had heard of my general zeal and intelligence to be merited, that I was a proper person to search Paris for Estelle Villebois.

That individual once found, a communication of the fact to Monsieur Achilles Blondel would not be a difficult affair. The desired result would follow of itself. I admitted the correctness of Monsieur le Millionaire's reasoning, and promised to use my best endeavours to discover the young woman. I stopped at that.

Had I given expression to a thought—a hope which flashed across my brain with respect to the original of the charming portrait in my hand, Monsieur Blondel would not have been so well satisfied or so liberal as he showed himself to be, when after mentioning two or three additional circumstances which might be of assistance to me, he, with lofty civility, wished me success, and went his way.

. . . . .

My highly-pleased friend at the Prefecture listened attentively to my report of the conversation that had passed between me and Monsieur Blondel.

"It is very well," said he, when I had finished. "You will endeavour to find Estelle Villebois, but your principal object will not be that. Listen. You know, by reputation, the Chevalier de Biron?" he then asked me.

"Certainly, I do."

"Well, he died four days ago, of wounds received during the Insurrection. He fought, I need hardly say, against the Reds; and there was no man in France who more possessed the intimate confidence of the illustrious Prince who, there can be little doubt, will be elected President of the Republic by the people."

"Prince Louis Napoleon?"

"Withour doubt, Prince Louis Napoleon. Well, the Chevalier de Biron was also an intimate acquaintance of Monsieur Achilles Blondel, and this spite of the very decided honest republicanism of the millionaire's spoilt son.

"The chevalier borrowed money of him, and died very considerably in his debt.

"Now, Le Biron, though poor, was a man of honour, of conscience, and finding that he could not live many hours longer, sent his friend, Monsieur Achilles Blonde the only valuable he possessed, a magnificent ecritoire, worth, it is said, intrinsically, ten thousand francs. It was a present from the Emperor Napoleon to the chevalier's father.

"The valet obeyed the dying man's order; the ecritoire passed into the possession of Monsieur Blondel, who a few hours afterwards presented it to Madame Alix the actress.

"Eh bien, in a secret recess of that ecritoire are confidential letters addressed to the Chevalier de Biron, which, in the hands of an enemy, would gravely compromise several individuals who stand high in Prince Louis Napoleon's favour. It is of the first necessity, therefore, to obtain possession of those letters—nine in number."

"That will not be difficult. Mademoiselle Alix will be easily bribed or bullied into giving them up."

"You are mistaken, my friend. She would be sure to mention the matter to her lover—her husband, that is to be, it seems; and he I have said is a Republican, and he would deem it a crime not to publish the traitorous correspondence, as he would deem it; and in twenty-four hours, or less, after we applied to Mademoiselle Alix, every salon and cabaret in Paris would be ringing with it."

"How came it that Chevalier de Biron, so devoted an Imperialist, did not order the dangerous letters to be destroyed?"

"He did not think of them till about an hour before he expired, when he dispatched his valet to Count ——," one of his correspondents, to apprise him of the unfortunate occurrence. The count immediately applied to me, well knowing," said my facile friend, with a shrug and a smile, "that in politics I belong to the party of common sense, to the winning party, that is to say, and that I am shrewd enough to know that party will not be Cavaignac."

"I count, therefore, upon you, Duhamel," he went on to say; "I count, therefore, upon you, Duhamel, to obtain the letters quietly, without affording Mademoiselle Alix or Achilles Blondel any ground for suspecting that such dangerous documents as these letters were ever in their possession."

"That is a pretty task! besides, may not Mademoiselle Alix herself discover the letters?"

"That is but too possible. The secret drawer is, however, very cleverly contrived. She cannot suspect the existence of such papers; and you, my friend, must be quick with your work."

"Can you give me a hint as to how I can set about it?"

"Ah, yes; Monsieur Blondel has lent you a portrait of Estelle Villebois, as I advised him to do. Very well; take that portrait to a clever artist, and have it copied, with this difference, that the girl's dress be not the same. Let also the copy be set in less expensive fashion than this, with which Blondel the younger is no doubt familiar. Eh bien, Estelle Villebois has an uncle, Jean Villebois, a seafaring man, whom Achilles Blondel never saw; Blondel senior is quite sure of that, and of that uncle the young man has heard the girl speak with affection. It also fortunately happens that no letter has ever passed between Estelle's mother and Achilles Blondel, who is, I must tell you, of a wonderfully plastic, tender, most effusive disposition. Comprenez vous, un peu?"

"I do not comprehend in the least. He will not be likely to conceive a tendresse for me, I suppose?"

"That is precisely what he will do for Jean Villebois, the uncle in whom Estelle was so much attached, and who brings him a letter from Madame Villebois, written on her death-bed with a sadness, a grief of temper, softened by the mother's remembrance of poor Estelle's love for him to the last, and her, Madame Villebois's, but re, cent discovery that he, Achilles Blondel, had not been to blame, but that, like her child, he had been the victim of a harsh father's cruelty. She consequently sends him her forgiveness and blessing, well knowing that by so doing she expresses the sentiments which the daughter· whom she humbly trusts to meet in Heaven befere thar letter meets his eye, entertained for him to the very last.

"Mon Dieu!" exclaimed my friend, with almost a shout of gratulation at his own cleverness; "Mon Dieu! Achilles Blondel will take the uncle of his lost Estelle to his heart at once. You will weep, embrace, condole, carouse with each other. He assures you that it is Estelle whom he loves in Mademoiselle Alix, which it appears is a fact; you express a wish to see, to be introduced to her He readily complies. You are charmed with the lady, who perceives that you are esteemed—have influence over her rich admirer. You visit at her lodgings with him—without him in a few days, when the lady is at a morning rehearsal, with a message from her lover, which you wait till she returns to be delivered, and l'affaires est faite! You obtain the letters; M. le Comte —— is grateful, and if sacre bleu, you can also succeed in finding Estelle Villebois, you will have gained a little fortune! C'est gros jeu, my friend, and you are sure to win."

"I don't know. I shall try to win, you may depend. There is one thing at all events of which I make sure. If I do succeed in finding Estelle Villebois—and not, I hope, in the position Blondel supposes (he has no proof that the betrayed girl has fallen into infamy), but whether so or not, I shall acquaint her with the millionaire's past conduct and present plans regarding herself; tell her that Achilles Blondel, whilst mourning her as dead, cherishes her memory with undiminished tenderness. Estelle

Villebois may be Madame Achilles Blondel. Who knows?"

"You have carte blanche in that respect. Now to the artist. The portrait, and Madame Villebois's letter, the composition of which you, following the line I have traced out, will, I know, manage very well—let Adrienne copy it (Adrienne was the cleverest copyist attached to the Prefecture)—the portrait, I say, and Madame Ville bois's letter, will be proof unquestionable that you are the genuine Jean Villebois. Try to bring me the letters—nine letters, remember—within a week, not later, if pos sible. Au revoir."

. . . . .

A young man of generous impulses, was Monsieu Blondel. It was difficult to believe he could be the son of the Millionaire Blondel, to whom gold was God. Perhaps his mother was a woman of fine nature, wedded to her husband, after the fashion of French marriages by the fiat of her father and mother.

I found him in a billiard-room, Rue de Chaillot, leading out of the Champs Elysees Avenue. He was sufficiently sober, but the ravages of intemperance were but too visible in his white, wasted face, which flushed scarl whenever he caught the eye fixed upon him of auyone who knew what he had been—should then be.

He played worse than indifferently. His shattered

nerves deprived him of all billiard skill. He was a sad wreck. The supposed suicide of Estelle Villebois was killing him, soul and body! Yet was he not so stricken vitally, but if that black burthen could be removed, the depressed springs of life might soon regain their old elasticity and force.

He lost every game, and at the conclusion of one I accosted him, and requested to speak with him for a few minutes privately.

Drawing himself haughtily up, and thoroughly scanning me, he demanded my name, and what possible pretence I could have for wishing to speak privately with him.

"I am Jean Villebois, the uncle of this beautiful unfortunate ——" I answered, in a low voice, showing him the portrait suspended round my neck.

The cue he held dropped from his hand; he staggered as if struck with a poniard, steadied himself by grasping the billiard-table, whilst his quivering gaze rested, as if chained by an irresistible fascination, upon the portrait.

"Have the kindness, Monsieur Blondel," I said, still softly and respectfully, and taking him by the arm, "have the kindness to pass with me into the adjoining apartment. I have a communication to make which may console you."

He yielded silently, and we were presently together alone.

I explained—the reader must bear in mind, or I shall fall very low in his or her estimation, that I was acting a part by command—I explained why I had sought him; he listened like one in a dream, and I concluded by reading the letter pretendedly from Madame Villebois.

Subdued, overcome by that voice from beyond the tomb, as he believed, Achilles Blondel, whose lymphatic, effusive temperament my patron at the Prefecture had correctly described, broke into passionate, sobbing lamentations, cast himself on his knees, kissed my hands, and adjured all things holy to witness that he had never been unfaithful, even in thought, to Estelle. In a little while he grew calmer, and we talked together.

"But I had heard that he had proposed to marry Mademoiselle Alix." Quite true, but solely because the lady resembled Estelle—faintly, imperfectly resembled her—as a dull, flawed mirror would reflect a purely beauteous image! I should like to make the acquaintance of Mademoiselle Alix. He would introduce me that very afternoon—say at five o'clock precisely, one hour before she left for the theatre, and when she would certainly be at home.

"We indulge in no illusions," said Monsieur Blondel, with extreme bitterness of tone; "we indulge in no illusions. Mademoiselle Alix is fully informed of Estelle Villebois's tragic story, distinctly understands why I sought her society, why I have determined that my father, who destroyed your angel niece, shall not gain the reward of the inexpiable crime by allying himself, through his son, with the Faubourg Saint Germain. I shall live, die' a drunken husband of a second-rate actress at a minor theatre—*will* live the drunken husband of a secon-rate actress of the Varietes! Ah! ah! that is revenge, if you like! You will agree it was scarcely worth while to murder Estelle Villebois to arrive at such a result as that!"

The last sentences were uttered in a hard, menacing voice, as if he were in present altercation with his father. The next minute, subsiding into the imbecility rather than the tenderness of tears, he wept aloud.

"I sometimes fancy," he murmured, apologetically, after awhile, "I sometimes fancy that drink, dissipation, has weakened my brain, never a very strong one. There is always a singing, a buzzing in my head, which explodes from time to time in sharp detonations, or I Imagine so."

"Evil symptoms, Monsieur. Precursors of paralysis—apoplexy. You are killing yourself."

"The farce will the sooner be played our. Oh! ıf I could but believe, as did that tender mother, who felt sure that she was about to find again, to rejoin the lost Estelle, to bask forever in the sunshine of her unfading loveliness. Illusion! Folly! The dream—a fast-fading dream now—of mankind when in their infancy: Estelle and her mother are now as they were a hundred years ago; their imaginary heaven is Neant. A pitiless anathema has blighted the world from the beginning—if there ever was a beginning—and will blight it to the end, if there shall ever be an end."

"Monsieur Blondel, excusing my frankness, will permit me to say, that if that second, third, fourth, fifth hand rubbish, rhodomontade, be not mere affectation, there must be more foundation than I am willing to believe for the fear that dissipation has weakened his brain."

"Perhaps. It is certainly true that I drink to excess—terrible excess."

"No one that sees you can doubt that. It is a sad vice, which Estelle would have despised you for—if she could have despised a man to whom she had once given her whole heart. There is a question I wish to ask," continued I. "Were you rich, independent, as you now are, when you forsook Estelle, or—"

"I never forsook Estelle," he interrupted, with explosive passion. "Have you already forgotten the letter you have read to me? True, I was rich, independent, when I was separated from Estelle—but I knew it not; I knew not till too late, too late! Allons!" said he, consulting his watch, "it is close upon five o'clock. Let us away to Mademoiselle Alix of the Varietes."

. . . . .

Mademoiselle Alix, though young in years, was a thoroughly practised woman of the world. I could not help fancying that I had seen, conversed with her before ; but concluded that that impression was caused by the patent fact that in form of features, in the colour of her hair and eyes, in all but the expression of sweetness, purity, and candour which illumined that charming face, she strikingly resembled the portrait of Estelle Villebois. Her carriage and conversation would, I daresay, be seductive, fascinating to novices, who could not recognise the stage-mannerism of the one—the flippancy of the other. She had certainly managed to enthral Achilles Blondel, and equally manifest was it that she despised the unobservant gull—that his sole attraction in her eyes was his wealth.

If I had little difficulty in correctly appreciating Mademoiselle Alix, she had none at all in detecting Theodore Duhamel, mouchard, under the guise of Monsieur Jean Villebois, captain in the mercantile marine of France. The annoying fact was, that about two years previously, Mademoiselle Alix had been implicated, not gravely, in a police affair I was employed to investigate, and she remembered me perfectly.

My recollection of her—I think I spoke with her only once—was, as I have said, uncertain, indistinct. Not only did Mademoiselle recognise me personally—but being cognisant of my vocation, she, for reasons to be presently developed, shrewdly guessed my motive in seeking an introduction to her.

It was not her interest to immediately unmask me. On the contrary, it instantly occurred to her that she might make effective use of Theodore Duhamel for the furtherance of a scheme on which her wits had been engaged for some days past.

The caressing condescendence of the lady towards Monsieur Jean Villebois, uncle to the amiable Estelle, whose sad history Achilles had made her familiar with, was somewhat overdone. Still, no definite suspicion of her purpose could, because of that caressing condescendence, arise in my mind; and I accepted without misgiving her invitation to favour her with a call at any time I should be passing that way.

If she should chance to be out, and it suited my convenience to remain till she returned, her servants would have orders, as in the case of Monsieur Achilles Blondel, to defer to my wishss, obey my directions. I have since wondered I did not suspect that such an invitation, so exactly what I desired, might not be a trap.

I called the very next morning, fully prepared for work.

Mademoiselle Alix, said a servant, was at rehearsal. Monsieur would, perhaps, rest himself in the salon till she returned?

First inquiring how long it was likely Mademoiselle would be absent, to which question the reply was that nothing could be more uncertain—a quarter of an hour, two hours, it was impossible to say—Monsieur Jean Villebois elected to rest himself in the salon for about a quarter of an hour—he had no further time conveniently to spare—since it was just possible Mademoiselle might return in that time.

. . . . .

The ecritoire, a really magnificent affair, stood at about he centre of the salon, at the end of which was a recesst-div.ded from the apartment by heavy curtains of violet-coloured velvet. As soon as the servant had retired, I drew aside the curtain, and saw nothing in the recess but a heavy, high-backed velvet covered canape (sofa-bed).

That ascertained, I set to work without loss of time, opened the ecritoire, and, aided by the instructions I had received, quickly discovered the secret recess: an unsealed note was there, addressed Mesire Jean Villebois; *autrement*, Monsieur Duhamel, Mouchard, who was informed that the letters he was commissioned to obtain were safe in the possession of a friend of Mademoiselle Alix. The words were still dancing in zigzag lines before my eyes, the evidence of wh ch I could scarcely believe, when a light hand was placed upon my shoulder, and a light laugh sounded in my ear. Whirling sharply round, I found that the hand, the laugh, were those of Mademoiselle Alix, who had softly entered the apartment, unheard by me, absorbed by my pressing errand. Never, sacre bleu! was police agent more confounded than I was at that moment.

Mademoiselle Alix, throwing herself into a fauteuil, burst into eclats of almost hysterical laughter.

"It is very amusing, no doubt, Mademoiselle," said I, recovering my self-possession, and encasing myself in the brazen armour of official impunity. "It is very amusing, no doubt; but I, a police agent, which you knew yesterday as well as you do at this moment, peremptorily demand the nine letters you found in this ecri. toire, and have purloined."

"Pardon, Monsieur Mouchard," said she, with bursts' of mocking merriment between almost every sentence? "pardon, Monsieur Mouchard, who could help laughing It is quite true, as you say, that I knew yesterday who Monsieur Jean Villebois really was—who, once having had the privilege of seeing, could fail to recognise Mon sieur Theodore Duhamel?—but nous autres comedians always wait for the cue which calls us upon the scene at the proper ttme. In this tragi comedy, and in, I believe, the last act, that proper time is now, and now—en avant la grande musique."

"I must beg of you, Mademoiselle Alix," I returned "to speak in language I can comprehend. Where are the letters?"

"The letters, Monsieur Mouchard, are in the possession of a faithful friend of mine. They are enclosed in a sealed envelope; and if my friend should hear that I have been arrested, that I have disappeared, his instructions, which will be properly acted upon, are to forward them to General Cavaignac. That is checkmate to M. le Comte ——. Is it not?"

"I do not know that. General Cavaignac's tenure of power will last but a few months."

"That is my conviction, Monsieur Duhamel. But during those few months the writers of those letters may be sent to Cayenne. Few persons return, I am told, from that charming Cayenne. As for Blondel, the millionaire, to be but briefly divorced from his money bags would be the death of him."

"Do I understand you to say that Blondel, senior, is compromised by the correspondence you, Mademoiselle, have surreptitiously obtained possession of?"

"Gravely compromised. Well, Monsieur Duhamel, do you begin to understand that there must be compromise—*transaction* between the parties you represent and myself?"

"Admitting, hypothetically, that to be so—what then?"

"I will tell you frankly, candidly, what, with the cards I hold in my hand, is my game. First, I will describe the precise situation.

"You are employed by the Prefecture of Police to get possession of nine letters, addressed to the deceased to the Chevalier de Biron, which letters have very fortunately come into my possession. Do not affect surprise. No one should know better than you, that actresses generally know as much of what passes in the great offices as the heads of the offices themselves —sometimes more."

"That may be true. Well?"

"You are also employed by Blondel, senior, to discover Estelle Villebois, who his son believes has drowned herself in the Somme."

"You are a witch; but continue."

"Mademoiselle being discovered, is to supplant me, which she could easily do, with Achilles Blondel."

"You are a witch, I repeat. Go on."

"I shall not surprise you when I say that, except for his money, I care nothing about Achilles Blondel?"

"A blind man might see that."

"Achilles Blondel does not see it. Till I had lit upon those letters, I took excellent care that he should not see it. Now he may wake to the truth as soon as he pleases."

"Riddle follows riddle. Pray explain."

"Willingly. To begin; Estelle Villebois is—is—guess! Come, I will give once—twice—thrice, twenty times to rightly guess what."

"I fear to guess aright the first time. Mademoiselle Villebois is one of the unfortunates, who, with cruel irony, are called 'fille de joie.'"

"Calumny, M. Duhamel. Estelle Villebois is—is—well, I may as well tell you, for you would never guess—Estelle Villebois *is my sister*"

"You lift me off my feet. Estelle your sister?"

"My sister. My hal -sister, that is to say. We are daughters of the same mother. My actress name is an assumed one. That to which I am entitled is Lemaire—Estelle Villebois and my mother's maiden name."

"Estelle Villebois and your mother's maiden name! That is a sad confession for a daughter to make."

"Not at all! Marie Lemaire, you will please to understand, was wooed, everybody believed, pour le bon motiff; was married with the sanction of her friends—her relations, to Victor Brettel. My mother—not knowing—was the best, the tenderest of wives—as I have heard my father a hundred times, in gusts of remorseful rage, defiantly assert in the presence of his detested, but lawful wife."

"His detested, lawful wife?"

"Oui, Monsieur Duhamel—his detested, lawful wife: Ah! twenty-one years have passed away since then, and I was but four years old; yet I well remember—"

"Pardon, Mademoiselle," I interrupted, having a strong suspicion that I was being, for some reason or other, outrageously mystified, "twenty-one and four make twenty-five; and you cannot be more than twenty, the age of Estelle Villebois, your half-sister."

"It is a compliment, Monsieur Duhamel, to my skilful care in preserving that which, frankly speaking, is the sole fortune of an actress—her youth and good looks. It is a sad verity, nevertheless, that the measure of my life is twenty-five years. I repeat that I was four years old when a coarse Creole woman, the wreck of a beautiful bad girl, whom Victor Brettel, intoxicated by youthful passion, had married on the Island of Martinique, suddenly presented herself at our place near Amiens. The Creole, whose legal right it was impossible to dispute, was at last forcibly expelled the house, and Victor Brettel left for Paris the same day, taking me with him, in spite of my mother's piteous supplications. His wife followed, and though he changed his name, she was not long in finding us out. They sullenly agreed to cohabit, and chiefly by her, I, poor helpless waif, was educated—drilled for the stage. She died about six years ago, having long survived her husband. They live in my memory, combined with only hateful, repulsive associations."

"You were not permitted to see or communicate with your mother whilst either of them lived, I presume?"

"No; the Creole, who had thoroughly subdued me to her tyrant will, was not cold in her grave when I left Paris for Amiens. My mother, the recently widowed wife of Captain Villebois, who had married her with the full knowledge of the past, received me with the tenderest kindness. So did Estelle. I remained until I could no longer remain to share the stagnant monotony of their lives. Having vegetated with them for nearly a month, I came back, in fulfilment of my destiny, to Paris."

"In presence of such remarkable frankness, I feel myself compelled to follow so excellent an example, by asking why, for what purpose, Mademoiselle Alix condescends to favour me with so interesting a chapter of family history?"

The concluding sentences, not yet narrated or recited by Mademoiselle Alix of that chapter, will furnish the explanation.

The following completes the narrative of her memorable career:—

"When Madame Villebois, and poor Estelle, upon he fresh morning of whose life so dark a cloud had arisen, left Amiens to shelter, hide themselves in the multitudinous obscurity of Paris, they naturally called upon me.

"I received them, I hardly need say, with the greatest cordiality.

"Estelle's rare beauty—her natural grace, which lessons could never teach—and docile aptitude, would, I saw, be an acquisition to the stage.

"I proposed that career to her. She consented; but soon that pure, sensitive nature, recoiled from actual contact with the realities of a profession which I need not tell an individual of Monsieur Duhamel's experience could not but wound the susceptibilities of such a maiden as Estelle Villebois.

"Eh! Mon Dieu, I admitted all that in my own mind. Still I was annoyed, piqued—enraged even. My amour-propre was outraged.

"There was a quarrel—a bitter quarrel—the bitterness, I confess, mine only.

"Estelle, with her and my mother, left in anger, and with insulting insolence, as I considered it, and which, a true child of my father, I cruelly resented; preferred semi-starvation in a garret to the comparative abundance they might have shared with me.

"At this moment they are earning scanty bread by needlework—embroidery, I am told.

"My intimacy with, as they believe, faithless, perjured Achilles Blondel, has made the gulf between us impassable till now. The conflict in my mind has been incessant, terrible," added Mademoiselle Alix, with much feeling, "and yet, but for the thrice fortunate finding of those letters in the Chevalier de Biron's ecritoire, I fear—nay, I am sure, I should have taken base advantage of the opportunity to enrich myself, which that intimacy, skilfully brought about, affords.

"I am as far off as ever, Mademoiselle Alix," I remarked. "How in the name of all the saints in the calendar, can the possession of these letters influence the situation?"

"I will tell you in a few words," she replied, and continued thus:—

"Achilles Blondel, by a formal deed, has secured to me (to me, the semblance of his lost Estelle) every franc he may die possessed of)—and he will not, his dissipated habits persisted in, live long—the sole condition being that I marry him!

"Egregious folly! Absurd infatuation, no doubt;

but the truth, nevertheless. Now I love—ardently love —money."

"That one can easily believe—the love of money is universal. I should like to know who does *not* love money!'

"Yes, and I love, truly love, my mother and sister, and I do *not* love Achilles Blondel. I pity him, it is true; and I believe my dear sister Estelle would rescue him from the abyss of degradation into which he has fallen."

"I also believe she would," I remarked, with sincerity."

"Eh bien! Monsieur Duhamel, the possession of those letters—the power which nothing can take from me of placing them in the hands of the actual Dictator General Cavaignac—enables me to reconcile my love of money, my determination to, by almost any means, secure a competence, with my duty towards my mother and Estelle."

"Indeed!"

"Indeed. Those letters, as you know very well, gravely compromise men who will have a splendid future before them, when the events which the writers plot for—namely, the accession of Louis Napoleon, first to the Presidentship, next to the Imperial throne of France—shall have been accomplished. The millionaire, Monsieur Blondel, is, perhaps, more deeply compromised than any other correspondent of the Chevalier de Biron. Well, for one hundred thousand francs——"

"One hundred thousand devils!" I exclaimed, with the most incredible surprise.

"For one hundred thousand francs, paid down in gold rouleaux—not one sous less—I write an order to deliver the packet of letters to you. My offer refused, the letters shall be in General Cavaignac's hands before that refusal is an hour old. Monsieur Duhamel, I have said my last word. Au revoir!"

. . . . .

There was no help for it, and I was glad there was not. My influential friend at the Prefecture, who, I afterwards knew, would have been gravely implicated had the letters not been recovered, instantly closed with the terms proposed.

Monsieur Blondel, the millionaire, advanced the money (a bagatelle, which the second Empire soon enabled him and his friends to recoup a hundred times over).

Mademoiselle Alix received the coveted rouleaux; the letters were delivered up; and the curtain fell upon the "petite comedia," as far as I was directly engaged therein.

I know, however, that within a week of the day when the actress of the Varietes so successfully achieved the "transaction," as she pleasantly called the exchange of nine letters for one hundred thousand francs, two marriages were celebrated at the Church of Sainte Genevieve. One, that of Estelle Villebois with Achilles Blondel, the father—how prevailed upon, I cannot say—assisting; and Mademoiselle Alix, *alias* Lemaire, with Theophite Beaumont, a musical composer of about her own age.

THE END.

CPSIA information can be obtained
at www.ICGtesting.com
Printed in the USA
LVHW040428110522
718423LV00002B/418

9 783375 004781